IVAN

and the
Moscow Circus

IVAN
and the
Moscow Circus

Myrna Grant

Christian Focus Publications

For Cookie, Donna,
Linda, Ed, Ron
and Eugene.
For friendship.

Copyright © 1980 by Myrna Grant
Republished in 2001
This edition published in 2006
by Christian Focus Publications Ltd.,
Geanies House, Fearn, Tain, Ross-shire,
IV20 1TW, Scotland
www.christianfocus.com
ISBN: 978-1-84550-135-8
Cover design by Andrea Raschemann
Black and White illustrations by Jos. E DeVelasco
Printed and Bound in Denmark
by Nørhaven Paperback A/S

Myrna Grant has travelled widely in what was the Soviet Union
and has experience of writing for children's TV and radio. She
is now an associate professor in communications at Wheaton
College, Illinois. She has many published works.

CONTENTS

A Chance Meeting

There was a pleasant slamming of compartment doors all up and down the train. The shrill whistle of the platform man signaled the 'all clear' for the train to resume its slow journey toward Moscow.

Ivan leaned back against his seat with a slight smile and closed his eyes. He was pretending to be a seasoned traveler, weary with the routine of the journey, a trifle bored with the delay of the train as it stopped at small villages to pick up a chance passenger or two.

Actually he was loving every minute of the journey and was glad there was still a long way before pulling into Yaroslavsky Station in Moscow where Momma and Poppa and Katya would be waiting to greet him.

It wasn't a journey he had wanted to make. A courtesy visit to distant relatives hadn't seemed like much fun when Momma and Poppa suggested it, but it had been a long time since Poppa's family in Vologda had been visited. A new baby had been born to a cousin Ivan didn't even remember, and Momma wanted to send along a special gift for the baby's first birthday.

At first the whole family had planned the journey together, but in the end it was decided that Ivan would go alone. Poppa did not receive permission from his supervisor at the factory to have time away from his

7

job, and Momma's factory's quota was increased so that there was extra production and longer hours to work in order to reach the goal. Katya begged to be allowed to go with Ivan but Momma was firm.

'You would be too restless on the long journey, Katya. And it is too much responsibility for Ivan to keep you out of trouble.'

Katya folded her arms indignantly and looked so innocently outraged that everyone laughed. Finally, even Katya smiled and plopped into a chair, playfully pouting at having been made to change her mood.

'I do not get into trouble!' she declared from the depths of the chair. 'It's possible that things happen to me from time to time, but that is the result of a lively and inquisitive nature.'

'Oh, indeed?' Momma tilted her chin at Katya thoughtfully.

'Yes!' came the muffled insistence. 'My teacher Valentina Semionovna says it is a fine thing to have a lively and inquisitive nature.'

'She didn't think it so fine when you got lost at the Science Exhibit,' Ivan declared, giving one of Katya's fat braids a pull. 'I didn't hear her praising you then!'

A pillow came flying from the chair, barely missing Momma's prized samovar on a table by the couch. Momma caught the pillow with a shake of her head. It was best for Ivan to make the journey alone.

Ivan felt the train lurch to a start. At the same moment, the compartment door opened and a battered suitcase was pushed through the door, followed by a boy Ivan's age. Ivan sat up straight with a smile.

'Hello!'

The strange boy hoisted his suitcase to the overhead rack, sat down on the bench opposite Ivan, and arranged his plastic bag of food on the side of the seat away from Ivan before answering.

'Hello.' He immediately stared out of the window.

Ivan continued to look at him for a moment. The boy was nicely dressed and had slightly long hair. He had a smooth complexion and lustrous dark eyes. Perhaps he is from Georgia, Ivan guessed.

The boy looked sad or sullen. Ivan couldn't decide which, but he began to feel uncomfortable at the boy's silence.

'Going to Moscow?' Ivan asked.

The boy turned his head to Ivan. 'Of course.'

Ivan shrugged. 'Me too.'

The boy was looking out of the window again.

'My name's Ivan. Ivan Sergeivich Nazaroff.'

The boy continued to gaze out of the window for so long Ivan was afraid he wasn't going to speak again at all. Finally with a sigh, he turned his head again. 'I am Volodia Petrovich Dyomin.'

Ivan smiled encouragingly, but Volodia turned again to the window. Ivan shifted in his seat uneasily. His companion clearly did not wish to talk. It was obvious he wanted to keep to himself. Such unfriendly behavior in a Soviet train was so unusual Ivan began to regret that the boy had come to his compartment. People always passed the time on trains talking, laughing, eating together. Another person in your compartment meant a new acquaintance, the exchange of stories, the sharing of meals, someone with whom to enjoy the passing view.

It's a good thing Katya isn't here, Ivan thought,

wishing suddenly she were. She would have filled up the silence with many questions. Katya would have paid no attention to Volodia's unsociability. Of course if Momma were here, she would have restrained Katya, whispering to leave the boy alone. Then, Ivan knew, Momma would have silently prayed.

Ivan looked more closely at Volodia. Although his body was tense, Ivan could see he was athletic and sat with an uneasy grace. A slight frown was creasing his forehead and from his profile, his sad expression seemed anxious, as if he were thinking very hard about a difficult situation.

Ivan leaned back again against his seat and closed his eyes. 'You can always pray, son.' How many, many times had he heard Poppa say those words? From as early as he could remember, in times of disappointment or frustration or worry, when it was true that nothing at all could be done about some problem in the church, some sorrow at school, some injustice, Poppa's advice was the same. As Ivan prayed, he could sense Volodia relaxing. He shifted and sighed and Ivan could hear him changing his position. When Ivan opened his eyes again, the boy was looking at him.

Ivan smiled.

Volodia nodded.

Ivan took a deep breath and sat up. 'I think it must be time to eat!'

'Of course,' Volodia agreed politely. 'I ate just before coming to the train. But you have been traveling a long time?'

'Four or five hours. From Vologda.'

Ivan opened the large bundle of food his Aunt Sophia had carefully wrapped in newspaper for him.

There was a large chunk of black bread and some cheese, hard-boiled eggs, sausages, and a tightly capped bottle of mineral water. Ivan offered the bundle to Volodia. Volodia shook his head quickly. 'Truly, I ate just a little while ago.'

Ivan paused to thank the Lord for the food and for the new friendliness of Volodia. 'Let me help him, Lord, if I can,' he prayed.

'Well, go on! Don't hesitate on my account. Really, I have just eaten,' Volodia encouraged.

Ivan took a bite of bread and chewed it thoughtfully. 'Are you going to Moscow to take part in some sports event?'

The boy laughed, his face lighting. 'No. Why do you ask that?'

'I thought you looked athletic. I play soccer and hockey for my school.'

Volodia nodded his respect. 'So you are how old?'

'Almost thirteen.'

'Ah. A loyal Young Pioneer, of course?'

Ivan suppressed surprise at the question, although he was suddenly on guard. Why would Volodia ask if he were a member of the Communist Young Pioneers? Almost every student in Russia, except those disqualified because of misbehavior or children with religious beliefs, belonged to the organization. As a Christian, Ivan had never belonged, in spite of the pressure of his teachers. But it was most unusual for a passing acquaintance to mention such a thing.

Ivan shrugged casually. 'Well, that's a good question.' It was an evasive answer showing he didn't want to discuss it.

'No?' Volodia looked suddenly interested. 'You

are not a Young Pioneer, I think, yet you are in sports? Something wrong?'

Ivan smiled. 'Nothing is wrong. At least, not with me. But you are right. I am not a Young Pioneer.'

Volodia shot out the next question. 'Why not?'

Poppa and Momma had taught Ivan that the Bible instructs Christians to be ready to give an answer to anyone about their faith. A direct question requires a direct witness. 'Although it is against the law to try to persuade people to be Christians, it is always permitted to answer questions,' Poppa would say.

Ivan paused a moment to choose his words carefully. 'Well, you know how it is. I am a believer.'

Volodia's dark eyes were alive with curiosity. 'A believer?'

'In God. In Jesus Christ. A Christian.'

There was silence in the compartment as Volodia thought about what Ivan had said. His response came slowly. 'I thought only old women...' His voice trailed off. Volodia frowned, bit his lip and started again. 'I've heard about religious believers.' He dropped his voice. 'I've heard such people still exist in our Soviet society, although they are mostly old women. But sometimes they are not.'

Ivan grinned. 'As you see,' he said.

Volodia did not return Ivan's smile. 'Is it true that sometimes religious believers are sent to prison camps or to hospitals for the insane?'

Ivan began to feel frightened. How could an ordinary boy like Volodia know such things unless he had some contact with the Secret Police?

Volodia suddenly stood up and pulled his suitcase down from the overhead rack. 'See this?' he asked

12

brightly, pointing to an emblem sticker on his suitcase. It looked familiar and Ivan bent forward to read it.

'I am a member of the circus,' Volodia declared proudly.

Ivan was amazed.

'Have you never gone to the circus?' Both boys were staring at each other in mutual surprise.

'No.' Ivan tried to be tactful. 'It is not the custom for believers to go to the circus. But I have sometimes wished to go.'

Volodia heaved his suitcase back on the shelf and sat down.

Ivan offered him some cheese and this time Volodia accepted. Ivan cut off a chunk with his pocket knife and handed it to Volodia with a question. 'What do you do in the circus?'

'I am an acrobat. And I sometimes help in the clown acts.' Volodia wiped his mouth with the back of his sleeve. A look of sadness passed over his face. He looked as if he wanted to say something. Ivan waited. 'I didn't mean anything by the question about your not being a Young Pioneer,' he said finally. 'I'm not crazy about the organization myself. In fact, even though I am fifteen, I'm not a member of the Komsomol.'

'Why not?' It was Ivan's turn to risk a question.

Volodia gave Ivan a steady look. 'Should I tell you everything about myself?'

'I told you I am a believer.'

Volodia raised a quizzical eyebrow in agreement. 'Let us say perhaps there are those in my family who have some differences with the politics of our government.'

Ivan glanced out of the window. A surge of

appreciation for the openness of his new friend warmed him. Outside, the pale spring green of the central Russian plains slipped effortlessly by. A turn of the head to the compartment door showed it was tightly closed.

When Ivan made no answer, Volodia continued. 'Especially an uncle of mine. An uncle I love very much.'

Ivan reached out to touch Volodia's arm. 'I am sorry.'

Tears glistened in Volodia's eyes. His voice was so low Ivan had to lean forward in his seat to catch what Volodia was saying.

'Is it true what I have heard about some religious people? Sometimes they are sent away…'

Ivan interrupted quickly. 'Yes. Sometimes…'

'In camps?'

Ivan nodded. 'Only certain very active leaders. Or believers who are outspoken. Or sometimes it is just a matter of an official who wishes to pass his time making trouble for some believer.'

Volodia stared hard at Ivan. 'And in hospitals? Are Christians ever sent to psychiatric hospitals…' His voice was a whisper. '…for the insane? When they are not – insane in the least?'

Tears now flooded Volodia's eyes. Embarrassed, he looked out of the window as he regained composure.

Ivan leaned over in his seat and grasped Volodia's shoulder. 'I understand, my friend. It is your uncle who has been put in such a place. But why?'

'He has criticized the government. He has had terrible trouble. Interrogations. Lost his job. And now…they have taken him to a special hospital where he is without rights. Possibly they are giving him treatments.'

Volodia stood up again and paced briefly in the swaying compartment. When he sat down his face was hard. 'But you could not understand what it is like to have someone you love in such a place.'

Memories flooded Ivan's mind. Volodia stared at Ivan's face.

'You do know,' he said softly.

Ivan smiled faintly in resignation. 'I do know. Once a pastor I loved was taken away to such a place.'

'Yet you smile.'

Ivan answered slowly. 'For believers, too, it is very hard. But for us, it is also an honour. Only the best of us suffer in these ways for Jesus Christ.'

A playful grin flitted over Volodia's face.

'Jesus Christ? But really, Ivan, isn't he a mythological character?'

Underneath the train, sparks flew as steel streaked across steel. In the compartment above, Ivan began to talk.

Homecoming

It wasn't that Volodia didn't listen as Ivan told him about Jesus Christ. It was simply that he didn't believe a single word. He liked Ivan's story about Jesus going about doing miracles, and interrupted with a folk tale his grandmother had told him about a peasant who was taken on a wild ride through the sky by a flock of cranes. Ivan had to listen politely. When Volodia finished his tale with a laugh, Ivan shook his head. 'You don't understand,. What I am telling you is true. Jesus did give sight to the blind-'

'And walk on top of a lake and turn water into vodka.'

'Wine!' Ivan corrected hopelessly.

'Oh yes, wine, and shout at the wind and make it disappear.'

But Volodia grew thoughtful. 'And for these harmless stories, and for talking in prayers to a god – excuse me, Ivan – who doesn't exist, people serve long sentences in prison camps and are sent to hospitals for the insane? It doesn't make sense.'

'Unless there is a God,' Ivan answered. 'Unless he is real and has real power.'

Volodia agreed. 'Yes. I suppose then it would make sense. There can be only one power in the Soviet Union: the government!'

'What did your uncle do that was so bad?' Ivan asked after a moment.

Volodia's expression grew gentle. 'He is a poet, my uncle. He wrote poems that the government doesn't like. They told him to stop, but he wouldn't. Many people read his poems even though the government won't let them be properly published. People copy them from pieces of paper and pass them along. More copies are made in this way. Many people read his poems,' Volodia repeated.

'I love poetry.' Ivan wished he knew how to ease the misery on Volodia's face.

'I have to get my uncle out of that place!' Volodia suddenly clenched his fists. 'He won't be able to stand it.'

It was an impossible idea. Both boys knew it.

'At least I've got to see him.'

The train slowed its speed to pass through a small village of wooden houses and rutted roads. In the small backdoor gardens early flowers and first leaves of plants pushed tenderly through the muddy earth.

'Does he ever get to go outside?' Ivan asked. 'To walk around the grounds?'

Volodia shrugged. 'I don't know. It's possible. In nice weather, surely they let people get fresh air and have visitors.'

'Perhaps we could figure something out,' Ivan offered. 'There's got to be a way...'

Volodia's face wrinkled in puzzlement. 'You would help me?'

It was Ivan's turn to use Volodia's favorite expression. 'Of course.'

'But why? You hardly know me. You could get into trouble.'

Ivan shrugged. 'I hope not.'

'But why?'

'Who else will help you?' Ivan wasn't sure he could explain to Volodia. He looked out of the window for a moment before answering. 'I've been around. Christians have a hard time in Russia. I understand.'

Volodia looked skeptical.

'The Bible says we are to do good to all men,' Ivan tried again.

'The Bible!' Volodia repeated the word so loudly Ivan looked anxiously at the compartment door. 'There are no Bibles in Russia! How would you know what was in the Bible?'

Ivan shook his head as he laughed. He used Volodia's proper name. 'Vladimir Petrovich, there is so much you don't know.'

'You have a Bible?' Volodia demanded.

'My father has one. They are hard to get, it is true. But there are ways.'

'To get a Bible? In Russia? I don't think so!'

'Well, it's true. And anyway, about helping you. Believers are often in trouble, or in danger of some trouble. Well, there are those who are experienced in figuring out ways…to help.'

Volodia looked more cheerful than Ivan had ever seen him. 'Do you really mean it?'

'I mean it, Volodia. It is a great wickedness to lock up perfectly healthy people in hospitals for the insane. Of course we must try to help your uncle.

I can't promise that we will succeed, but we can try, and pray.'

'Whenever I had a vacation from the circus, I lived with my uncle,' Volodia said in a rush. 'I have no parents. My mother died when I was a little boy. My father died last year, after I had started with the circus. My uncle is…all I have…' He lapsed into silence.

The train was nearing Moscow. There was activity in the corridors. People began clogging the passageways, calling good-byes to new friends they had met on the journey, making their way to their own compartments to gather their belongings, to smoke, and await the end of their journey.

'We are coming to Moscow!' Volodia looked unhappy.

'It's all right. I will come to see you,' Ivan reassured him.

'Come to the circus!' Volodia commanded. 'A week from tomorrow. At six o'clock, before the performance. We will have time to talk then.'

Ivan felt a sudden panic. 'You mean, come and see the circus?'

Volodia laughed. 'Of course! I will get you in free. It would endanger you if I were to try to come to your apartment. As the closest relative of my uncle, I suspect I am watched. It might endanger you if I visited you. But for a boy like you to come…it would mean nothing.'

'Well…to help someone…I'm sure it would be all right.'

Volodia laughed. 'How strange you Baptists are. So brave and yet so timid. What do you think would hurt you at the circus.'

'It's not that,' Ivan replied with dignity. 'It's that we believe that worldly entertainment – excuse me, Volodia–'

Volodia nodded his pardon vigorously.

'But we wish to please God in all that we do – not to be distracted from thinking of him…and loving him. Our parents and pastors teach this.'

Volodia looked mystified but not in the least hurt. 'If you cannot come to the circus, I understand.'

Ivan shifted in his seat. 'I will come, of course. To see you…to help your uncle. If I tell my parents you need my help, they won't mind.'

A mischievous grin lit Volodia's face. 'But you won't stay to see the circus? You won't stay to see me do my act?'

The train was slowing to a stop. Volodia became busy getting down his large suitcase.

'Of course I will see your act!' Ivan tried to hide his excitement. 'You are my friend, aren't you?'

Volodia suddenly hugged Ivan. 'What a good person you are, Ivan. I am very glad we met today – even if nothing comes of our plans.'

Doors were slamming up and down the care with glad finality as the train eased to a stop. The corridor was full of people pushing to get off the train.

'From Dserzhinkskaia Square you can get a number 13 trolley bus to the circus,' Volodia said in a rush. 'Or a number 24 bus past Red Square. Can you come a week from tomorrow night?'

Ivan nodded. 'Yes, I think so.'

'Come to the side door on the right of the building as you face the ticket office,' Volodia commanded. 'There will be a sign to the left of the door. It says 'The Administration of the Moscow Circus.''

Ivan felt suddenly embarrassed. 'Are you sure? I could buy a ticket.'

Volodia was opening the compartment door. 'It's only one ruble ninety kopecks for a good seat. Don't be foolish. Come to the side door and ask for me. I'll wait for you there. About six o'clock? It's better if we don't get off the train together.' Volodia parted with a hasty handshake and disappeared into the crowd of irritated passengers who tried to push together to impede his progress toward the front of the car. But Volodia easily made his way through, smiling so winsomely at the people that some actually made a path for him.

Ivan took his place in the line. To think he would see the circus! And to know someone who performed. A flush of guilt reddened his cheeks. He hoped Momma and Poppa would understand!

At home, Momma had prepared an especially good welcome-home dinner. The borscht was steaming and Momma plopped a larger than usual spoonful of sour cream in the middle of Ivan's bowl and handed it to him with a smile. Poppa listened with pleasure as Ivan told the news of his relatives and described the festivities celebrating the new baby's birthday. Katya's eyes danced with excitement as Ivan recounted the family details. But soon enough it was time to tell about the train ride home and the strange boy who had shared his compartment.

When he had finished, there was silence around the table. Ivan felt intensely uncomfortable. It had come out wrong, he thought. It sounded as if he thought himself a great hero, offering to help Volodia. It was an impossible idea. And to go the circus! Ivan glanced nervously at Momma. He knew she would disapprove. His eyes moved to Katya's face ablaze with hope. Perhaps if Ivan got to go to the circus, somehow she would be able to go also. Ivan knew what she was thinking and he looked down at his plate.

Finally Poppa cleared his throat. 'That's quite a story, Ivan.'

'Perhaps I was foolish, Poppa,' Ivan offered. 'Perhaps it was very wrong to offer to help Volodia. But he was so worried…'

Momma poured more tea in Ivan's glass. She reached out her arm and lightly smoothed Ivan's hair. 'It's a terrible, a horrifying thing, to put healthy people into psychiatric hospitals. It is only natural to want to help.'

Poppa sipped his tea. 'As you know, Ivan, sometimes a Christian brother is put into such places. The state knows very well there is nothing wrong with the minds of our brothers. It is to terrify them into denying the Lord. It is to put a stop to the Christian work they are doing…the influence they might have with others.'

Ivan began to feel more comfortable. 'I know. I told Volodia.'

'It is a far worse thing than sentencing believers to the camps. In the camps only the body is imprisoned. But in the hospitals the mind is attacked.'

Momma looked thoughtful. 'Volodia's uncle, he is not a Christian, Ivan?'

Ivan shook his head no.

'It must be even more dreadful for people to go through such experiences without the help of Jesus.' Momma's lashes glinted with tears.

Katya's bright face was also clouded. 'But the Lord is with our pastors and believers who suffer in such a way.'

Poppa smiled at Katya. 'Certainly.'

'Then, Poppa, I may go to the circus to see Volodia?' Ivan asked.

'And me too? If Ivan goes, I may go too?' Katya hunched her shoulders excitedly.

Momma exchanged a doubtful glance with Poppa.

'It is the safest way for Ivan to meet with Volodia,' Poppa spoke thoughtfully.

Momma nodded slowly. 'I suppose so.' She turned to Ivan. 'But Ivan, it isn't going to be possible for you to really help Volodia see his uncle. If the doctors forbid visitors, then there is no way.'

Ivan agreed quickly. 'I know, Momma. But if Volodia and I can talk more, perhaps an idea will come.'

'Yes.' Poppa stood up with a sigh and reached for the Bible he kept on a shelf next to the table. 'It is a blot on our country that people are unjustly put in such hospitals.'

Katya pulled her chair next to Poppa's and pulled his arm around her. 'People are sent there by our courts because they displease the government or the police?'

Momma shook her head. 'It is a terrible thing.'

'How do they ever get out?' Ivan asked.

Poppa opened the Bible. 'They are declared cured when they agree to change their own thinking, or be silent.'

'Don't some people pretend?'

'I suppose so,' Poppa answered. 'But of course when they leave, if they continue to write or speak in the old ways, then they are put in the hospitals again. There is little point in pretending.'

They were reading the Gospel of John, and Poppa began the account of the wedding in Cana. When he came to the part where Jesus told the servants to fill up the wine pots with water, Ivan remembered how Volodia had called the wine vodka, and he smiled.

A Thrilling Performance

Ivan had not wanted to bring Katya to the circus. Momma had not wanted Katya to go. Even Poppa had wrinkled his brow thoughtfully when Katya begged to be allowed to go with Ivan to meet Volodia.

'We won't be wasting our money,' Katya pleaded. 'Volodia will let us in the side door and we will be his guests!'

'It's not a matter of the money, Katya.' Poppa pulled Katya's long braid thoughtfully. 'You know as Christians we have a responsibility to spend our time as well as our money in the best possible way.'

Katya was good at teasing. She was good at pestering questions that never stopped until she got an answer. She was good at tagging along after Ivan. But Katya hardly ever begged. If Momma or Poppa said no, then Katya was usually able to understand the reason for the decision. Ivan had almost never seen the look that had filled Katya's eyes. It was desperate.

'Please, Momma, Poppa. I've never seen a circus. I won't ask again. Just this one time.' Katya shot a look of urgent pleading in Ivan's direction.

Ivan relented and cleared his throat. 'Maybe it would be good to have Katya along,' he volunteered slowly. 'It would look more as if I were just there with my sister to see the circus if anyone was suspicious about Volodia talking to me.'

Katya held her breath, staring first at Poppa and then at Momma to see the effect of Ivan's words.

Finally Momma shook her head with a little sigh. 'It's all right with me if your Poppa approves.' Momma got up from the chair where she had been mending an apron. 'I'm going to start dinner.'

Poppa rubbed his hands together. 'I'm hungry!' He looked at Katya's reddening face with a grin. 'I think you ought to take a breath, Katya. You're going to need to be able to breathe when you go to the circus!'

Katya had thrown herself rapturously into Poppa's arms. 'Oh, thank you, Poppa!' Over his shoulder her shining eyes found Ivan with a look of sheer gratitude. Ivan laughed.

'She'll have to behave herself,' Ivan told Poppa gruffly, pretending not to be enjoying Katya's delight. But Katya was off into the kitchen to hug Momma, and a clatter of spoons on the floor and a burst of laughter told Ivan and Poppa she had made an impact.

But now, knocking far more bravely than he felt on the modest side door of the immense Moscow circus building, Ivan wondered if it had been a good idea to bring Katya.

'Knock again!' she was urging. 'You didn't knock loudly enough, Ivan. Nobody heard you.

Shall I knock?'

'No, Katya,' Ivan said with exaggerated patience in his big brother voice. 'Someone will come.' He stared at the gold letters chiselled into black marble at the side of the door: 'Moscow Administrative Headquarters.' It looked impressive and not at all like a circus door. Just as he raised his fist to bang more

vigorously, the door was pulled open and Volodia's cheerful face appeared. He raised his eyebrows at Katya.

'My sister,' Ivan explained.

'Good, very good!' Volodia pulled them both inside with a sweep of his arm. 'You're late. I want you to see the beginning of the circus. That's something!'

Prodding them violently from behind Volodia rushed Ivan and Katya through clusters of people clogging the halls in colorful disorder. There was a blur of costumes, electrical cables, music, and the unfamiliar smell of stage make-up and perfume. Suddenly Ivan and Katya found themselves seated very comfortably in the audience in one of the front centre rows.

'Oh, Ivan!' Katya gasped.

The lights of the circular auditorium dimmed. A massive film screen began to be lowered slowly from the high ceiling. The orchestra stuck up a booming patriotic march. As soon as the screen was in place, pictures flashed on its surface in rapid succession, matching the rhythm of the music. Red Square on May Day, flags flying, crowds cheering, soldiers marching, Sputnik streaking toward the heavens, the happy faces of farmers waving from their yellow tractors, school children with their bright red scarves, arms filled with flowers, marathon sports events from Moscow's Dynamo Stadium, all flashed before the audience's delighted eyes. And from the centre entrance to the ring, the performers began to march out carrying huge flags. Acrobats in brilliantly colored tights, animal trainers leading bears and elephants, clowns riding cycles, bareback riders balancing on their beautiful horses – the movement, the color, the singing of the performers transported the audience.

Grow, become mature,
young country and your people;
None are happier than you in all the world!
The earth for us is a peaceful circus ring,
And it is the youth who come out into this ring!

Some of the audience joined the performers in the refrain:

We celebrate our youth;
We celebrate all its sixty years.
We celebrate our beautiful Motherland!

Then the song continued:

The Soviet Circus brings out its art
Like a flag of friendship of common man.
We devote our thoughts and feelings to you,
Motherland of Lenin's ideas!

Ivan glanced down at Katya sitting on the edge of her seat, her face rapt with delight. The children exchanged excited smiles as the song finally ended and the flags and the performers swung through the entrance out of the circus ring.

A tremor of anticipation swept through the crowd in the silence that followed the last strains of the music. The movie screen ascended rapidly to the ceiling. Suddenly a spotlight flashed on two clowns, so famous that even Ivan and Katya

29

had heard the names and seen pictures of Rotman and Makovsky. The orchestra struck up a lively rendition of Prokofiev's Romeo and Juliet as the clowns, seemingly unaware of the audience, began their celebrated act. The first clown had a trowel and began making exaggerated digging motions with grand sweeps of his arm, bending over a bit of the ring that was meant to be a garden. As he dug, he produced a cheerful plastic flower, 'planting' it in the earth and singing thoughtfully,

A king goes to war singing with his men,
But when he returns there are no men!
He lost the war, he lost half his leg,
But he was glad to be alive!

The second clown, forgotten in the shadows outside the spotlight, suddenly jumped into the light, his king's crown slightly askew. Comically chasing the flower-planter and terrifying him with menacing gestures, he eventually tore up the flower and threw it across the ring. The music was now tumultuous. Weeping, the first clown returned to his flower plot and picked up the trowel he had thrown down. Another period of digging, and another bright plastic flower was drawn from the depths of his clown costume and devotedly planted in the earth. Again the music swelled and wavered ominously, and the king clown reappeared. Katya grabbed Ivan's arm in excitement. This time, the flower clown picked up a spade and defended his flowers. There was a gasp from the audience as the angry king clown drew from under his cloak a round black bomb with a large 'A' painted on the side in white. The music reached a peak of tension and suddenly the whole circus theatre was plunged into total darkness. There was silence for a moment and then the lights blazed. Every eye was on the small flower patch. Nothing remained but the bomb, a bone, and the king's crown.

After a moment, into the spotlight danced the flower clown once more as the music changed into a lighter, happy tune. The clown picked up the bomb and planted it where the flowers had been. Flourishing a bright watering can, he watered the bomb, and from the top of the bomb a flower slowly emerged. The orchestra ended the act with a triumphant fanfare. All the houselights came up to feature Rotman and Makovsky, now in the centre of the ring, bowing gaily. The audience went wild with the stamping, rhythmic unison applause that expressed the highest enjoyment and thanks.

As the applause resounded through the auditorium, circus workers ran into the ring carrying huge mats that they unfurled with amazing speed. Before their eyes, the ring, which Ivan guessed to be about thirteen metres across, was prepared for the art of a female trapeze artist. Katya held her breath in terror as the woman flew through the air under the high dome of the auditorium. Once or twice Katya tightly closed her eyes as the woman released her hold on the swinging bar and soared for the high arc of a second bar swinging from the opposite side of the ring.

Everything in the circus was done with such speed and expertise that the children had no time to feel impatient for the appearance of Volodia. In fact, Ivan had almost forgotten that his new friend was actually a performer in this amazing world of music and color, speed and comedy. With a gasp, Ivan grabbed Katya.

'It's Volodia!' he cried, staring with amazement at the youth proudly standing high under the circus dome on a small platform. Volodia's name was called out by the ringmaster, who announced he would perform the amazing triple somersault in midair. To the orchestra drum roll, Volodia leaped into the air, swinging back and forth on the bar until he had gathered enough speed. There was a flash of his blue costume, like the plumage of some graceful bird in flight. The audience gasped in admiration as Volodia's body doubled over again and gain in three somersaults. At what seemed to be the last possible instant, Volodia effortlessly grasped the free swing bar with both hands, whipped his body over it and sat swinging on the bar like a child on a playground swing. The applause was deafening. Ivan was bursting with pride, laughing and clapping and stomping his feet wildly.

Katya clapped until her hands stung. 'Oh, Ivan, he is the best of all!' she cried above the applause. Ivan agreed. There was no one in the circus like Volodia.

The next act was six brown and six white horses doing precision manoeuvres, responding to the slightest direction from their uniformed riders. They were decked in colorful harnesses and streamers and made delicate turns and sudden formations, galloping, cantering, lifting their legs high in imitation of a dance. The children loved the high tossing of their heads, the glorious shine of their bodies and the amazing way such powerful creatures could swerve, turn, retreat, and zigzag in swift patterns of pounding hooves and flashing color. Too soon it was over and the last applause died away. People quickly shrugged into jackets or sweaters against the cool spring night air and made their way to the exits. Fathers carried sleepy children in their arms.

Ivan and Katya busied themselves in their seats, buttoning their sweaters and trying to appear to be leaving.

'Where's Volodia? What should we do?' Katya whispered, looking around her seat as if she might have dropped something

'I'm not sure,' Ivan answered slowly. 'We came in such a rush...'

'Quickly! This way!' Volodia's voice behind them was so unexpected the children jumped.

'Volodia! I didn't see you!' Ivan grinned at his friend, but his greeting was cut off.

'This way!' Volodia was speaking urgently. 'Something important has happened.'

An Exciting Discovery

It was a pleasant room to which Volodia hurried Ivan and Katya, a small sitting room next to a row of dressing cubicles. Once inside, Volodia locked the door.

'Any of the performers may use this room,' Volodia explained. 'No one will bother us if the room is locked. There are many such rooms.'

'You were wonderful, Volodia,' Katya said shyly. 'I've never seen anything so beautiful, but I was so afraid you would fall when you did those somersaults!'

Volodia smiled in appreciation. 'You should have seen my father! He was a master acrobat!' Volodia's face changed as he turned to Ivan. 'Something important has happened about my uncle.' Volodia looked anxiously at Katya.

'She can keep a secret,' Ivan reassured him. 'Don't worry about Katya.'

Volodia shrugged. 'There is a news correspondent who years ago used to be a friend of my uncle. They read poetry together. Then the journalist was returned to his own country. Now he is back in Moscow. I saw him in the audience tonight. He is my uncle's friend!'

Ivan looked skeptical. 'He won't be able to get in to see your uncle. The authorities would never let a newspaper man into a psychiatric hospital. And did you talk to him?'

'No! Of course not!' It was Volodia's turn to look skeptical. 'I thought you understood about these things, Ivan. It would not be possible for me to approach him. It would be suspicious if anyone saw me. The nephew of Alexander Ivanovich is talking to a foreign correspondent? You must be crazy.'

'Then what good is it that he has returned?'

'You must go to see him, Ivan! You must tell him of the injustice to my uncle. A perfectly sane man is put into a psychiatric hospital because the government doesn't like the poetry he writes. Because the government says he must be crazy to disagree with any policy of the government.'

Ivan nodded. 'You think the journalist might write a story about your uncle and send it out to the West? And people in the West would protest?'

'It is possible. He was my uncle's friend'

'What's his name?'

'Halvor Nyborg. He is Norwegian.'

'And he speaks Russian?'

'Certainly!'

'Where does he live?'

Volodia gave Ivan a quizzical glance. 'Of course I don't know. I didn't talk to him.'

'Then how am I supposed to find him?'

Volodia rubbed his legs with the palms of his hands. He gazed out of the window at the night sky. He looked back at Ivan. 'You said you knew about these things,' he answered finally. 'Perhaps there are people in your church – other people who know other correspondents...' he finished weakly.

'Volodia,' Ivan's voice was strained. 'We Baptists don't know newspaper people. We wouldn't dare to know correspondents from foreign countries. We meet pastors and sometimes church leaders from the West who come to Russia as tourists, but I don't know anything about how to contact journalists. And to try to find a particular foreign journalist – well, you know that is dangerous. People find out. People ask why.'

'But you said you would help me,' Volodia challenged.

Katya nodded vigorously. 'Of course we will help you, Volodia. Ivan just means he can't think of a plan right now!' Katya cast a furious glance at Ivan. 'Ivan likes to plan everything very carefully.'

Volodia slapped Ivan on the back in relief. 'Good! Very good! It is a fine thing to think out exactly what to do.'

Ivan cleared his throat. 'Katya's right, Volodia. I will help you. Right now I can't think what to do. But there is a text in the Bible, 'With God, all things are possible.' I'll count on that.'

Volodia smiled. 'Ah, the Bible again. The walking on the water. The wonderful stories. Well, perhaps your God will make a wonderful story out of your finding my uncle's friend.'

'He does make wonderful stories, Volodia,' Katya said softly. 'You should hear some of the stories of what God does. I know some good ones.'

Volodia gave Katya a gentle look.

'And not from the Bible!' Katya added quickly. 'I mean what he does today for people who ask him.'

Volodia took a piece of paper out of a small pocket notebook and scribbled on it. 'This is the name of the newspaper my uncle's friend used to work for when he was in Moscow before. Perhaps this will help you find him. But the best thing would be to go to events where the foreign press might be. You know – the opening of exhibits, or perhaps foreign artists who come to perform in Moscow – things like that.'

'How will I know him?' Ivan scratched his head. 'What does he look like?'

'Oh, he looks very Norwegian,' Volodia asserted. 'He has a beard and a round face and looks very strong. He has reddish hair.'

Ivan tucked the piece of paper deep into his shirt pocket. 'Shouldn't be too hard.' He pulled down the corners of his mouth in mock casualness. 'Moscow is only a city of four and a half million people and has thousands of foreigners living here too. Shouldn't be too hard to find one Halvor Nyborg, a foreign correspondent with a reddish beard.

'Ivan!' Katya rebuked her brother. 'This is serious.'

'Yes, it is serious,' Ivan agreed with a steadying look at Volodia. 'And I will pray and ask God to help us. I will start tomorrow trying to find this Mr. Nyborg. Perhaps Poppa will have some ideas.'

Volodia hugged Ivan in the Russian way as he locked the door. 'Thank you, Ivan. You come to this door any time in the early evening and ask for me. Someone will call me.'

In an instant, Ivan and Katya were in the cold night air, hurrying to the bus stop. The evening had been so full, so strange to each of them, the children were absorbed in their own thoughts as the bus came and they mounted the steps and sat down. The woman fare-collector smiled as she approached them. 'At the circus?'

Ivan gave her the fare and nodded.

'It was wonderful!' Katya smiled at the unexpected friendliness of the woman.

'You're very late,' she observed.

'We have a friend in the circus,' Katya chatted, oblivious to the slight look of disapproval on Ivan's face.

The woman sat down wearily in the seat in front of them as the bus lumbered through the streets. Only a few other tired passengers slouched in seats throughout the bus.

'I like a good time,' the woman said. 'Of course when you are young, that is the time to enjoy yourself.'

Ivan nodded politely.

'I don't go out at night. I work,' the woman stated. Then she shrugged and laughed at the obviousness of her remark. 'If I had my evenings free, I know what I would do right now. I would go to the American exhibit. Did you know there is an American exhibit on Herzen Street? It is an exhibit of American home industry.'

The children listened politely. Ivan was thinking about the bearded Norwegian and Katya was remembering how Volodia looked as he somersaulted through the air.

'Perhaps you don't think it would be an interesting exhibit,' the conductress continued, 'but it is. Do you know what they have there?'

Ivan shook his head.

'They have American kitchens, refrigerators and stoves and lots of small appliances. I'd like to see that!'

It wouldn't be possible to go to the Norwegian embassy, Ivan thought. No Russian citizen could go to a foreign embassy. Soviet police guarded the gates.

'It's very crowded, the American exhibit. It's been open a week but lots of people who go can't even get in, the lines are so long. It's not worth missing my sleep to stand in line for that! I have to sleep during the day.'

Katya yawned. Suddenly the thought of sleep was very appealing. She snuggled into Ivan with a weary sigh.

'But of course tomorrow it will be terrible there.' The bus lurched to a stop to let a passenger off. No one got on, so the conductress continued her conversation. 'Tomorrow there is to be a reception by the Moscow Department of Industry. No one will get in, you can be sure. Television people, newspaper men, government officials, that's who will get in tomorrow.'

Ivan sat up so suddenly Katya almost slipped off the seat into the aisle.

'Be careful of your sister,' the woman reproached mildly.

'Tomorrow the press is going to be there?' Ivan demanded.

The woman looked surprised at his interest. 'That's what I said. But you won't get in, if that's what you're thinking.'

'Newspaper people?'

'I suppose so, yes. That's what happens at those receptions. Foreigners, television people, people with pull, they are the ones who will be there. But you wouldn't see anything at all if you go. It will be too crowded.'

The woman rose to her feet as the bus slowed down again to pick up a solitary person waiting at a brightly lit stop.

'But I would like to see an American kitchen someday.' She tapped the back of the children's seat with her ticket punch as she passed. 'That's what I'd do if I had an evening free.'

Katya was still feeling too happy to scold Ivan for almost knocking her off the seat. 'Why did you keep asking her questions, Ivan? Who cares about an industry exhibit?'

'Katya!' Ivan's voice was tight with excitement. 'Don't be so stupid! Aren't we looking for a newspaper man?' He said the words so quietly Katya could barely hear.

Her eyes widened in excitement. She clutched Ivan's arm. 'You said you would trust God, Ivan! Oh!' Her voice trailed off in wonder.

Ivan pulled Katya to her feet. 'Our stop,' he said cheerfully to the conductress. She nodded as the bus ground to a stop and the door wheezed open. Ivan jumped down and helped Katya off. 'Wait till we tell Momma and Poppa!' he grinned. 'With God all things are possible!'

An Unexpected Visitor

All the next morning in school the hours seemed to drag endlessly. Time after time Ivan thanked God that it was Saturday and that the afternoon was free. It seemed to take forever for the children to get home, eat their lunch, and make their way by bus to Herzen Street and the exhibit. Poppa had read in the morning edition of Pravda that the official visit was to take place at 3 p.m. The children would have plenty of time to be there before the news people would arrive.

All the same, Ivan pushed anxiously through the mobs of people outside the exhibit. Ahead in the crowd he could see television cameras mounted on high stands, ready to take pictures of the event. In every direction were militia soldiers, and circulating through the crowds were the plain clothes men of the KGB Secret Police, instantly recognizable to any Russian citizen.

'I don't see any foreigners!' Katya exclaimed breathlessly. Ivan jabbed her so sharply in the ribs she gasped. But she did not protest. She blushed. It was a foolish thing to say aloud in a Moscow crowd.

People were asking questions and shoving each other for a better view of the entrance to the exhibit hall. Many were passers-by who, seeing the excitement, had joined the crowd in hopes that perhaps something scarce was being sold. Some hoped that by a stroke of fortune, they might be able to gain entrance to an event of such obvious interest. Ivan's ears were straining to hear any western accents or foreign languages. Usually foreigners grouped together, even in crowds, Poppa reminded him.

A strange expression hit his ears. It was perfect Russian, but the way in which the words were strung together in the sentence sounded odd. Ivan wheeled about, listening intently for a repetition of the voice, his eyes scanning the crowd for western-looking clothes that might signal the presence of a foreigner.

A woman with a string bag bulging with new books pushed into Ivan. The books banged into the side of his leg, causing him to pull away in pain. The woman advanced through the crowd, her chin high, trying to see over the heads of the people in front of her.

'Katya,' Ivan began, feeling almost ready to give up what appeared to be an impossible search.

Katya was nowhere to be seen. Ivan stood still, looking in all directions for a glimpse of Katya's brown braids and soft white ribbons.

There was a flurry as some official cars arrived on the street. The militia roughly pushed a way through the crowd for the arrival of some dignitaries. The men wore medals of merit and bright badges on their dark suits and they chatted easily with one another as they moved through the parting mass of people.

Ivan forced his way in one direction and then another, looking for Katya, but she seemed to have melted away. Some people tried to block Ivan with their bodies as he pushed forward. Some scolded him for his rudeness.

'I've lost my sister!' Ivan explained. 'I'm trying

to find my sister!' The crowd grew denser as the television cameras started to roll, filming the arrival of more dignitaries. There was a scattering of applause somewhere in the crowd, but Ivan hardly heard it. 'Surely Katya could have stayed with me!' Ivan was struggling with a wave of exasperation. 'She knew very well I had to be watching out for foreigners! All she had to do was see that we didn't get separated!'

There was a tight group of photographers by the entrance to the building, shielded from the crowds by the militia. As more officials arrived, there was a scramble of activity among the photographers as they jostled in the confined space for better angles for their pictures. Ivan turned in another direction, pushing back through the press of people. Once in a while he caught a glimpse of a small brown head and struggled toward it, only to be disappointed. His anger grew to worry. What would Katya do when she couldn't find him? Surely she was working her way through the huge crowd somewhere, looking for him. He tried to remember if she had any kopecks for the ride home and if she would know what bus to take. She could probably ask someone if she didn't know. Would she go home? Would she stay in the crowd, trying to find him?

The brief ceremony held at the entrance of the building was obviously finished. Some people began working back through the crowd to the street to make their way home. Others joined the long line that circled the building in the hope of gaining admission to the exhibit.

Even in the thinning crowd, Ivan could not find Katya. Finally, with lips clamped together in

frustration, he strode to the bus stop. It was stupid to always have to bring Katya with him when he went out. This would be the last time he would take her anywhere, he promised himself. And he would probably get into trouble because Katya was lost.

With a sigh, he slumped into the seat of his bus. He had started out with such high hopes. Now he was going home, not only not having the slightest clue as to how he might find the Norwegian newsman for Volodia, but without Katya.

His heart was heavy as he dragged himself up the stairs of the apartment building and opened the door.

'Ivan!' Katya jumped up from the sofa.

'Finally! We thought you would never come home!'

Ivan glared at Katya in fury. 'I spent all afternoon looking for you!' he accused. 'Where were you?'

Momma drew Ivan into the room and shut the door. 'Ivan, we have a guest.'

Ivan looked at the chair in the corner of the room that was always used for company. A blond man was getting to his feet with a smile, extending his hand to Ivan.

Poppa put his arm around Ivan's shoulder. 'This is Ivan, our son we've been telling you about.'

The blond man took Ivan's hand and shook it heartily in the western manner. 'I'm very pleased indeed to meet you, Ivan.'

Ivan smiled more at the man's accent than in friendliness. He was still feeling very cross at Katya.

'Mr. Newell brought Katya home from the Industrial Exhibit,' Poppa explained. 'We were just going to have some tea, Ivan. I'm sure after your afternoon, you'd enjoy a glass of tea also.'

Ivan felt foolish. Everyone was behaving in such a polite manner, as if something very pleasant had happened, when the truth was, Katya had behaved very badly and everyone was ignoring it. Ivan didn't want tea. Ivan didn't want to sit down and chat with the foreigner and give in to the feelings of curiosity that were stirring in him. He wanted Katya to cry and apologize and he wanted Momma and Poppa to scold her. Instead, Katya was looking very pleased with herself and treating the foreigner as if he belonged to her.

'I looked everywhere for her,' Ivan said lamely as he sat down.

'I'm sure you did, Ivan,' Poppa said warmly. 'I'm sorry you had a bad time. It must have been very crowded.'

'It was crowded!' Ivan agreed. 'But I do think Katya could have tried to stay with me!'

'I did, Ivan!' Katya declared righteously.

She isn't even sorry! Ivan lifted a glass of tea from the tray his mother offered him and took his drink so quickly he burned his mouth. Choking he shook his head hopelessly.

'Don't be cross, Ivan,' Momma said gently. 'Mr. Newell is from Canada.'

Something in the way Momma said the word 'Canada' seemed to awaken Ivan. A foreigner! In their own apartment! Not in the street, surrounded by militia people curious to hear what is being said to an outsider.

Ivan ignored his stinging tongue. 'Canada. That's a very large country, like the Soviet Union.'

The stranger agreed. 'Yes. Our two countries are very much alike in many ways. Very large, with vast wilderness and lots of winter. You have Siberia. We have the North.'

'We studied Canada in school,' Ivan offered.

There was a pause. 'Do you play hockey?' Ivan asked

The man laughed. 'I suppose every boy growing up in Canada plays hockey. We had a rink near our house, and all winter everyone skated. It was just a small town where I grew up. There wasn't much else to do in the winter.'

'The girls? Did they play hockey, too?' Katya's eyes were sparkling with excitement.

Mr. Newell laughed. The corners of his eyes crinkled in a way Ivan liked. 'Oh, no! It was too rough for them. We used to fight over who would have the rink, though. If the boys were playing hockey, the girls just had to wait.'

'They should have taken turns,' said Katya primly.

Ivan laughed. 'Katya would like to be a boy,' he teased.

'I would not!' Katya blushed indignantly.

Poppa shifted in his chair. 'You will see, Mr. Newell, that boys and girls are the same in all countries. I think even in Canada, brothers like to tease sisters.'

Mr. Newell agreed. 'My sister is grown up and a writer now. I still like to tease her!'

Momma passed a plate of cookies to their guest. 'We are very grateful that you were so kind as to bring our Katya home. She could have found her way from the bus, but it was very good of you to see that she arrived safely.'

'You have a charming daughter.' Mr. Newell smiled at Katya. 'It has been my pleasure to meet her. And to meet your family. I think the most enjoyable part of working in a foreign country is actually meeting the people.'

Poppa nodded heartily. 'What work brings you to Moscow, Mr. Newell?' he asked.

Mr. Newell gave a warm look to the Nazaroff family. 'I hope you won't mind,' he answered. 'I am a journalist. I am a correspondent for a newspaper in Ottawa.'

A Secret Telephone Call

A chill ran down Ivan's spine. He stared at Mr. Newell in absolute astonishment. So many questions suddenly exploded in his mind, he was unable to speak.

Poppa noticed Ivan's reaction with puzzlement. 'Of course we don't mind, Mr. Newell,' Poppa answered, still looking curiously at Ivan. 'It must be a very interesting life, living in different countries and reporting for your paper in Ottawa.'

Katya was staring at Mr. Newell in delight. But she knew better than to speak. It was simple enough, she was thinking. The Lord knew they needed a foreign correspondent and he sent along Mr. Newell. But something in Ivan's face kept her quiet.

Mr. Newell's observant eye had caught Ivan's reaction. He leaned toward Ivan casually. 'Are you interested in journalism, Ivan?'

Ivan was trying hard to recover his composure. Could this man be trusted? Was it possible that he knew Halvor Nyborg, the Norwegian journalist? Was there some way he could help Volodia's uncle? 'I haven't really thought very much about it,' Ivan answered carefully. 'But of course I am interested. I suppose you meet lots of people. Other journalists…'

Katya gave Ivan an approving look.

'Oh, yes,' Mr. Newell agreed. 'We foreign journalists are pretty much kept together. It's meeting ordinary Russians like you that is a special pleasure.'

There was a slight awkward silence in the room. Katya suddenly grinned mischievously. Ivan knew she was thinking what good stories 'ordinary Russians' like them could tell: of the Church, said to be almost dead, and how it was growing. Of pastors who were in prison even though freedom of conscience was guaranteed in the Soviet Union. Of children taken away from their Christian parents because of religious influence. Of how much believers would pay for an ordinary Bible. Of people like Volodia's uncle.

Momma too had intercepted Katya's look, and she stood up. 'Thank you again, Mr. Newell, for your kindness. I think we must be detaining you from your work.'

Mr. Newell stood up quickly, giving Ivan another glance from the corner of his eye. 'Not at all, Mrs. Nazaroff,' he answered, reaching for his hat. 'As I said, it was a pleasure.'

Ivan's heart was pounding. He couldn't let Mr. Newell get away, but his mind was a blank. What could he say without telling the whole story? And if perhaps Mr. Newell was a Russian agent, watching the children after their visit to Volodia, Ivan would be falling into his hands.

Poppa reached to open the door and Mr. Newell caught his hand in a hearty handshake. 'Thank you for the tea and hospitality,' he began. He released Poppa's hand and slipped his own hand into the pocket of his light overcoat, drawing out a card which he handed to Poppa. 'I should be very glad to keep in touch with your family,' he said with a glance at Ivan. 'Perhaps we could meet sometime for coffee or a meal.'

Poppa took the card with a broad smile.

'Thank you. We in Russia have very warm feelings toward Canada.' Poppa opened the door, and in an instant, Mr. Newell was gone.

In the next few days, Ivan was more and more exasperated at himself for not speaking to Mr. Newell when he had the chance. What harm would it have done, he asked himself, if he had simply asked Mr. Newell if he knew a Norwegian journalist called Halvor Nyborg? It would have been simple enough to say a friend knew him. He wouldn't have had to say anything more about the friend. But instead, stupidly, he had said nothing. And now it would be very difficult indeed to make contact with Mr. Newell without his suspecting that something important was going on.

It was always a matter of extreme interest to the police when Soviet citizens had contact with tourists from the West. It was a matter of critical importance if an ordinary person visited a foreign journalist. It would most certainly be a matter for investigation if it were discovered.

One afternoon Ivan walked all the way to the Moscow River to think things out. A glint of pale

spring sunshine suddenly lit the churning waters of the river. Ivan often spent time at the river; it was his favourite place to be alone and sometimes to pray. Because today was a Sunday, many people were out walking along the embankment, enjoying the mild weather and the occasional bit of sun breaking through the windswept clouds overhead.

By law, Ivan could not attend church until he was eighteen, so for him, Sundays were days to be spent in quiet rest and relaxing. He tossed a stone toward the river and tried to see if it actually hit the water or fell before it reached its mark. It would be nice, he thought, to worship openly and regularly with other believers. The six years until he was eighteen seemed long.

Ivan fingered Mr. Newell's card at the bottom of his pocket. He had been pretty sure Poppa and Momma would not encourage him to contact Mr. Newell. It was important for Christians to be above suspicion, to do nothing to cause the police to think they might be disloyal Soviet citizens. Momma especially would worry if she thought Ivan was trying to find a Norwegian journalist. And if there should be problems, and Momma were ever questioned about Ivan's activities, it was best that she would be able to say she knew nothing.

On a sudden impulse, Ivan turned in the direction of a telephone booth in a nearby post office and began walking. His hand was shaking as he dialed the number on Mr. Newell's card. He had heard that all the telephones of foreigners in Moscow were bugged, and he knew he would have to be very careful. The ringing of the telephone seemed to roar in his ear, and Ivan had to fight down an impulse to hang up before anyone could answer. Perhaps no one would be at home on a Sunday, Ivan thought with relief.

The voice at the other end repeated the number and said, 'Hello.' Ivan wasn't sure that he recognised the voice. 'Mr. Newell?'

'Yes?' The reply was alert with interest.

'It's the brother of the lost girl you took home,' Ivan began.

'Oh, yes. Hello. Good to hear from you.'

Ivan was greatly relieved that Mr. Newell had not

used his name. Ivan took a deep breath. 'You said to keep in touch...'

'Of course! I'd like that very much. I'm not busy this afternoon.'

Ivan's heart gave a lurch. 'Uh...I'm not either, really.'

'Shall we meet then? Say where.'

Ivan couldn't think of a place. His mouth was dry with fear at what he was doing.

'How about Red Square? Is that too far for you?' Mr. Newell's voice was encouraging.

Ivan could see the golden domes of the churches from the window of the post office. 'No, that's good,' Ivan said firmly. Somehow he felt reassured. 'I'm near Red Square at the moment.'

'See you in a few minutes, then.'

Ivan held the telephone receiver in his hand even after the dial sound buzzed loudly from the instrument. Quickly he looked around as if someone might have overheard the conversation. Slowly he replaced the receiver. It had all happened so quickly. It was almost as if Mr. Newell had been waiting for him to call. Ivan felt both frightened and exhilarated as he strode towards Red Square.

'Well, Ivan,' Katya had once said to Ivan in a teasing way, 'if you're going to pray about things, you better expect answers!'

Remembering her words, Ivan grinned. He had prayed that he would be able to help Volodia's uncle in some way. It was true that he shouldn't be surprised at answers.

Revelation in Red Square

Ivan loved Red Square at any time of year, but it was especially exciting in fine weather. For one thing, tourists from all over the Soviet Union and the whole world flocked to the Square to join the long lines of people edging toward Lenin's tomb. Since 1924, Ivan's teacher had told his class, the body of Vladimir Lenin, founder of the Soviet Union, had been preserved in an open coffin for all to see.

For another, soldiers on leave from the Red Army were often roaming around the Square, taking pictures of St. Basil's Cathedral with its beautifully fashioned turrets, photographing each other by one of the great gates of the Kremlin Wall, stopping to listen to the famous chimes of the Spasskaya Tower.

On one side of the Square was Moscow's Main Department Store, a huge ornate building with its rows of glass windows. The inside reminded Ivan of an enormous greenhouse, with long aisles lined with crowded booths selling various goods. Bridges spanned the different sections of the store and a central fountain splashed torrents of water for the delight of tired shoppers.

On the other side of Red Square were the great walls of the Kremlin. Inside the massive gates were the ancient palaces of the Czars and the white stone cathedrals and churches of Russia's antiquity, their high golden domes glistening in the soft sunshine.

Red Square was the heart, not only of Moscow, but of the whole Soviet Union. But today Ivan was not watching the tourists or enjoying the sights. His eyes scanned the crowds, looking for Mr. Newell. He wasn't positive he would recognise him, and he knew he didn't have the faintest idea of what he would say. He wished he knew more about foreign correspondents. Could they always be trusted? He wondered if any were informers, men who would report to the government if anything unusual came up. From the few things he had heard, he didn't think so. For the most part, they seemed to be kept pretty much away from ordinary Russian life.

'Have some ice cream?'

Ivan wheeled around and almost knocked a paper of ice cream out of Mr. Newell's outstretched hand. Mr. Newell was grinning as he lifted some of his ice cream with the edge of his tongue.

'Thank you!' Ivan accepted the treat and fell into step with Mr. Newell as he began to stroll around the Square.

'Glad you called me. It's too nice a day to stay inside. It was a long winter.'

'Yes.' Ivan licked his ice cream.

'How are your parents? And Katya?'

'Fine, thank you. They're fine.'

There was a long pause.

'And you?' A gust of wind blew Mr. Newell's sandy hair into his eyes. He brushed his hair back and looked thoughtfully at Ivan.

'I'm fine...but I have a friend who's...looking for someone.'

'I see.' Mr. Newell pulled a camera out of his pocket and took a picture of St. Basil's. 'And I can help?' he asked as he snapped the picture.

'I don't know. He is also a foreign journalist, this person my friend is looking for.'

'Why does he want to find him?' Mr. Newell wound a knob on his camera and shoved it back into his pocket.

When Ivan didn't answer, Mr. Newell sat down on a nearby bench. Ivan joined him. They both gazed at the bright colours of the cathedral domes.

'Ivan, may I say something to you?'

'Of course.'

'I've met a few young people since I have been on assignment in Moscow and they are usually very curious about Canada and excited to meet a foreigner. They have lots of questions and I try to answer them. That's all there is to it. If we make friends, it's not a matter of trust because they merely want to chat with someone from a different country. But Ivan, I think you may be concerned about whether or not you can trust me. Perhaps it has to do with some problem your friend is having.'

Ivan scanned the crowds a moment before he answered. 'I suppose so.'

Mr. Newell stretched his arm along the back of the bench. 'I know I am a stranger, Ivan. But I'd like to help you if there is some way.' Mr. Newell pulled something out of his pocket so quickly Ivan was startled. 'Sorry.' Mr. Newell smiled, flipping open a wallet. 'This is my nephew in Ontario...Canada.'

Ivan saw a colour photograph of a teenage boy in a blue and white woolen cap and a heavy blue jacket. On the jacket was a large white maple leaf. 'His favourite hockey team is the Toronto Maple Leafs,' Mr. Newell went on. 'What I'm going to say now will sound strange to you, Ivan, but I'd like to say it anyhow. It's got to do with our being friends. In order for me to help you, you have to believe I am your friend.'

'I think you are a friend,' Ivan offered.

Mr. Newell's voice was gentle. 'But you need to know, don't you?'

Ivan nodded. 'If possible, of course.'

'Ivan, do you know that many people in Canada believe in God?'

Ivan's heart lurched. 'No, I wouldn't think so many.'

'But there are many. Most Canadians believe there is a God.' Mr. Newell stood up and began to stroll again. Ivan was glad of the change. His mind was racing with questions. 'Maybe they don't all go to church or to synagogue, but many do. Many are Christians and I am one of them.' Mr. Newell glanced at Ivan's flushed face. 'Do you know what that means?'

'Yes,' Ivan answered.

'I'm rather surprised. I'm glad,' Mr. Newell laughed with pleasure. 'But what I'd like to say is, Christians don't lie. They do keep their word. It's very important to them – and to me, because I am a Christian. That means when I say I am your friend and would like to help you, I mean it.'

A slow smile lit Ivan's eyes and spread to his mouth. 'This means you are my brother,' he said shyly.

Mr. Newell stopped walking and looked hard at Ivan. Then suddenly he hugged him. 'I don't believe it!' he cried. 'Ivan Nazaroff. I can't believe it! But I have never seen you at the Moscow church, have I?'

'My parents feel it is best if I wait to go until I am older,' Ivan answered. Suddenly the sky seemed to unroll in blueness. The crowds around him leaped with colour. All his uncertainty and discouragement melted into a wave of joy.

'Is this trouble to do with being a Christian?' In their excitement, Mr. Newell and Ivan were walking faster, passing out of Red Square toward the ornate old Rossya Hotel.

It took only a few moments to tell the story of Volodia and his uncle and the Norwegian journalist who had been the uncle's friend.

Mr. Newell's voice was low enough that no one passing could hear. He spoke urgently. 'Ivan, I have met Nyborg! But I'm afraid it's not very good news. He was actually sent by his paper to cover the American Home Industrial Exhibit where I met Katya. He was staying at a hotel in Moscow, but I think I remember his saying he was leaving this weekend.'

'Oh, no!'

'But perhaps I can find out what hotel and can go and see him, Ivan. I'd like to ask him what he knows about Volodia's uncle. It's not that I don't believe Volodia's story, but the more you know, the better. I think I ought to go back to my apartment and see what I can find out.'

'You do believe that sane people are locked up in mental hospitals? You believe this is done in our country?' Ivan asked urgently.

Mr. Newell's face was sad as he shook Ivan's hand in farewell. 'I've been a newspaper man a long time, Ivan. I do know. And I will help if it is possible. Do you know where the planetarium is?' he asked suddenly.

'Of course,' Ivan answered in surprise.

'Can you meet me there tomorrow about five? I'll tell you whether I was able to see Nyborg. It's better not to phone.'

'Until tomorrow.'

'And Ivan!' Mr. Newell touched Ivan's sleeve as he turned away. 'Pray.'

Ivan was singing softly as he made his way to the bus. A foreign Christian had reminded him to pray!

Dangerous Documents

Volodia swung lazily from hand to hand on the practice bars high above the ring of the Moscow circus. All acrobats learn that when practicing and when performing, everything must be put out of the mind except the trapeze and the readiness of the body to respond to split-second timing. Today he didn't feel like practicing. So many thoughts swam in his head, he knew his concentration and timing would be off.

Olga Valentinovna, a veteran acrobat with the circus, was watching Volodia with a sharp eye. 'Volodia!' she called up to him. 'What's the matter with you this morning? You're not concentrating.'

Volodia looked down at the tiny figure on the circus floor. A bar swung past him, almost hitting him on the head.

'Come down,' Olga called. 'Volodia, come down a minute.'

Obediently, Volodia released the bar and somersaulted to the net below, bouncing expertly to his feet and swinging over the rigid side of the net.

Olga tousled Volodia's hair. Putting an arm around him, she walked him to the side of the ring. 'You were able to visit your uncle yesterday, Volodia,' she said in a low, matter-of-fact voice.

Volodia was astonished. Olga had always been his friend, but he was frightened. He had told no one at the circus about his uncle.

Olga gave Volodia an understanding smile. 'Don't be worried. You ought to know that whenever there are…difficulties…in a family, the police come around asking all sorts of questions. It's nothing special.'

'The police were at the circus yesterday?'

Olga shrugged. 'Of course. Why do you think you suddenly got permission to visit your uncle? That was so you would be out of the way when they came around. You aren't supposed to know, of course, that there was an informal investigation of you.'

Volodia nodded in appreciation. 'Thank you, Olga. Thank you for telling me. I know this means I am also being watched.'

Olga shrugged. 'I have told you nothing. I don't know what you are talking about.'

Volodia grinned. He had always liked Olga. She had been almost a mother to him and now he liked her better than ever.

'Why don't you do some exercises this morning, Volodia? Stay off the bars until your mind is more settled. I can say I needed extra practice on the bars.'

Volodia nodded agreeably as some performers strolled by. 'Certainly I will trade with you, Olga Valentinovna. I can do some exercises in my room.'

As Volodia glanced over his shoulder, Olga was already snapping on the practice belt with the line fastened securely to pulleys at the top of the circus roof. With a tug on the rope, she indicated she wanted to be pulled up. Her graceful figure was soon swinging rapidly from the high bars.

Volodia jogged to his room and gratefully locked the door. He hadn't slept well all night and yet he had been afraid to turn on his light in case someone would see it and ask why he was not sleeping. What had happened during his visit to his uncle had been so dangerous his mouth still went dry thinking about it. Volodia had been permitted a fifteen minute visit with his Uncle Sasha in section four of Moscow's Serbsky Institute. Volodia had been given a pass from the nurse in charge and had been accompanied to his uncle's bed by a white-coated doctor. 'It is important that you persuade your uncle to cooperate with the doctors here and with his treatment. It is only as he recognises that he is in need of treatment that he will get better. You must convince him that we are the experts and understand these things.'

Volodia nodded his head nervously. He was afraid to say or do the wrong thing in case the doctor would suddenly decide to refuse the visit.

His Uncle Sasha was sitting up in bed with a worried smile on his face. 'Volodia!'

Volodia embraced his uncle fiercely. 'We have only fifteen minutes, Uncle,' he began.

'Quite long enough for a sick man!' the doctor reproved Volodia. He leaned against the end of the bed.

Volodia looked at the doctor, who was clearly posted at the bed, and then back indignantly to his uncle. The uncle shook his head gently to indicate that Volodia must not make a fuss.

'Uncle, how are you?'

'I am fine, Volodia. There is nothing at all the matter with me,' he said clearly. 'I sleep well, I eat well, I have a perfect memory for events and aside from the fact that I am in a madhouse, I have never been better.'

The doctor sighed loudly. 'It is not for the patient to make such judgments, Alexander Ivanovich,' he declared with patience. 'Here, of all places.'

'Here most of all!' Volodia's uncle's eyes suddenly flashed in anger at the doctor. 'Here most of all, the patients know better than the doctors the cause of their illness.'

'So you see, you admit that you are ill,' the doctor retorted.

Uncle Sasha closed his eyes in impatience. Volodia ached with frustration. He wanted to tell his uncle so much. But the doctor would not leave! And time was melting away.

'How are my friends?' Uncle Sasha swung his legs over the side of the bed away from the doctor. Volodia moved quickly to his side.

'Fine, Uncle. Our old friend, Comrade Nyborgsky may be in Moscow.' Volodia knew even though he had made the Norwegian correspondent's name sound Russian, his uncle would understand what he meant.

Without surprise, Uncle Sasha said, 'Good. I should like to see him. Perhaps he could visit sometime.'

'Only family may visit, as you know,' the doctor reminded.

'Of course,' said Uncle Sasha as if he had forgotten.

'And your birthday is soon, Volodia. If I do not see you, happy birthday.'

'Thank you, Uncle.'

'Your nephew wishes to encourage you to admit that you need treatment and to accept the judgment of the doctors here.' The doctor gave a stern look to Volodia.

Uncle Sasha smiled. 'Of course. Let us not waste time with all that, doctor. Put it in your records that my nephew sought to persuade me.'

Suddenly, in the bed directly across from Uncle Sasha, a patient leaped to the floor and started shouting. The doctor wheeled around. In that instant, Uncle Sasha swiftly pulled a small sheaf of papers from the inside of his hospital uniform and thrust them down the open neck of Volodia's jacket. Volodia's face went white and in spite of himself he began to shake.

The doctor turned again to Volodia and Uncle Sasha. The uncle had swung his legs out on his bed and was watching the performance of his fellow patient with amusement. Volodia was clutching the front of his jacket in fear.

'I insist that I be permitted visitors!' the patient was shouting. 'Every Sunday my wife, who is my next of kin, seeks to see me and every Sunday she is refused. Why? I declare this place is a madhouse!' The patient grinned mischievously.

Two nurses hurried to the man's side. 'You are disturbing the ward. You are frightening the visitors!' They pulled the man toward his bed.

'I am quite calm now,' he affirmed mildly with a slight twinkle toward Uncle Sasha. 'I merely felt the need to make a strong statement.' He glanced quietly around the ward. 'I do apologise for startling anyone here. It's only that I do miss my wife and I am here only because I wrote an appeal to leave the Soviet Union.'

Uncle Sasha grinned at the doctor. 'That's mad enough,' he joked.

'Your time is up,' the doctor said to Volodia disapprovingly. 'I think you might have tried harder to encourage your uncle to be more cooperative.'

'His visit has done me a lot of good,' Uncle Sasha replied. 'It was a wise treatment, doctor, and I have benefited.'

The doctor pulled Volodia's arm. 'The boy is still quite startled by the outburst.' The doctor glared at the patient who had shouted. Volodia gave the man a sudden shaky grin.

'Don't forget to search that young boy,' the patient called to the doctor. 'I've given him some secret documents.'

Volodia's heart almost stopped beating. Perhaps the man was mad after all! If an attendant searched Volodia, whatever his uncle had hidden in his jacket would be discovered.

The doctor shook his head as he escorted Volodia to the door. 'I do not have an easy job here, young comrade. That man claims to be here only because he has asked to leave the Soviet Union! Anyone who likes can leave! Secret documents! You can see he is mad!'

Volodia coughed politely to hide a smile in spite of himself. A nurse opened the ward door with a questioning look at the doctor. The doctor nodded him through. Volodia passed onto the street, his hands folded across the front of his jacket. What had his uncle given him?

Followed

At first Volodia thought his uncle had smuggled poems to him written at the Serbsky. But as he smoothed out the papers, he realised that what he had was the official report of the so-called 'psychiatric' examination his uncle had undergone at the hospital. It took Volodia only an instant to realise the 'D' stood for doctor and the 'A' for Alexander, his Uncle Sasha's formal name. Such examinations inside psychiatric hospitals were top secret, and Volodia knew what a powerful document his uncle had entrusted to him. He began to read.

D. Why were you hospitalised here?

A. I don't know. There is absolutely nothing wrong with my mind.

D. Couldn't it have some connection with your poetry?

A. My poems have nothing to do with mental illnesses.

D. But they contain remarks about our government.

A. What remarks?

D. I am asking the questions. What do you say about our government?

A. I am not interested in political ideas.

D. Whoever sent you here received a phone call about the ideas in your poems.

A. Whatever my views are, they have nothing to do with mental hospitals.

D. If that were so, you wouldn't be here. Just remember, you're not a famous poet. You can't expect publicity. For your remarks, you'll be kept in this psychiatric hospital as long as I say.

A. Then we have nothing to discuss.

D. Your ideas are critical of our Soviet government. They are crazy ideas. Until we have cured you, you won't be permitted to leave.

A. Then you admit I am here not because of any mental sickness at all, but only because of what I have written in my poems.

D. People are put in mental hospitals because they are a danger to society.

A. That is supposed to mean people who would hurt themselves or hurt other people.

D. Precisely. Your views are a social danger. Now you are beginning to understand.

A. I understand that I am a perfectly healthy man, locked up in a madhouse because of my ideas. There is absolutely nothing the matter with my mind, yet you told me I would have to be given medicines and other treatments until I was no longer 'sick.'

D. You think you know better than a doctor whether you are mentally well or not?

A. Of course I know I am mentally well. You know it too.

D. We are getting nowhere. You must see that your ideas are a danger to the state.

A. And my friend Dimitrov, who is in the bed opposite me, how are his ideas a danger? He is a simple Christian who goes to church and prays. He wishes to leave our country because his life is unlivable for him here.

D. We are discussing you, not Dimitrov.

A. His supervisor at his work reported him for answering questions about belief in God. His ideas too are a danger to the state?

D. Obviously he was harming our social way of life by attracting others to the church and to his religious fantasies.

A. But freedom of religious belief is permitted by the state.

D. We are discussing you and not Dimitrov, the believer.

Here Volodia paused in his reading and took the page to the window for better light. There were no more 'official' typed pages. There was a scribbled line from his uncle: 'Volodia, try to get this paper to the West. It will indicate that I am sane. They will not let me out unless I promise no more poems. I kiss you. Your uncle.'

A spring rain was pelting the glass of Volodia's window. The light became very bad. Volodia turned on a lamp and pulled a chair up to his table. He was churning with emotion.

Ivan at that moment was gazing out of his school room window, watching the same rain and thinking of his meeting at five o'clock with Mr. Newell.

'Ivan Sergeivich!' his teacher's voice drew his eyes quickly to the front of the classroom. 'I do not think you will find a great deal to inspire you staring at the sky. Unless, of course, you are taking the opportunity for a time of prayer.'

Ivan flushed. Several children in the class giggled. A few did not. They looked down at their books sympathetically.

'I'm sorry, Galina Petrovna,' Ivan responded.

'I would appreciate it if you would save your prayers for another time, Ivan Sergeivich,' his teacher continued. 'If there is some urgent assistance you require, perhaps you could consult me. You may find I have better hearing than the sky.'

At this there was outright laughter.

'I was daydreaming, Galina Petrovna,' Ivan tried to ignore the grinning faces turned toward him. 'It won't happen again.'

'Oh, daydreaming. I beg your pardon,' the teacher replied. 'But all the same it is not permitted. You will do an extra chapter of history tonight, Ivan, and write me a report for tomorrow morning.'

Ivan thought again of his meeting with Mr. Newell. Of all nights to have extra homework!

'Certainly, Galina Petrovna. Thank you.'

The rain was still pelting down two hours later as Ivan ran to the steps of the huge Moscow Planetarium. He could see a figure huddled in the doorway, dressed in an expensive-looking western coat. Ivan's heart lifted in gladness. He made a dash for the entrance, splashing so carelessly through the puddles that Mr. Newell laughed.

'You're soaked!' he cried as he shook Ivan's hand. 'Let's go inside and get some hot tea.'

Ivan wrapped his cold fingers around the amber glass of tea and breathed in the steam appreciatively. Mr. Newell bit into a crusty roll. 'I saw our Norwegian friend,' he began, his eyes twinkling with the effect he knew his statement would produce.

'You saw him' He is still in Moscow?'

Mr. Newell shook his head no in the middle of a gulp of tea. 'It was quite remarkable, really. I got to his hotel in time to help him carry his bags to the lobby. He was actually on his way to the airport. We went for a quick walk around the block.'

'And he knows Volodia's uncle?'

'Says he is one of the finest men he knows. A very good poet, apparently. Even had some of his poems printed in the West, although Nyborg isn't sure Volodia's uncle even knows this. Some poems were smuggled out by somebody. A good poet and a very sane man.' Mr. Newell put his glass down and gazed thoughtfully at Ivan. 'Now where do we go from here?'

'Couldn't you write a story about him for your paper? Perhaps people in the West would protest that

a person is locked up in a madhouse just because he writes what the government does not like.'

'Ivan, I am a journalist. I know from Nyborg that such a man, Alexander Ivanovich, actually exists and that Nyborg says he is a good man and confirms that he is a poet. I know from you that this poet has a nephew working in the circus, who is apparently his only relative. You tell me that this poet is locked up in the Serbsky Institute, a place for the insane. Those are not enough facts for a story. Perhaps the poet really is mad! Journalists cannot write stories on what other people tell them. They must have facts, proof.'

A feeling of helplessness engulfed Ivan. His spirits, so high only a few moments earlier, plunged. He stared at his empty tea glass. He did not notice a man watching the conversation from a nearby table in the museum restaurant.

As Ivan sighed, the man rose from his place and made his way to the table where Ivan and Mr. Newell sat. Casually he pulled up a chair. 'Excuse me, Comrades. May I join you for a moment?' he looked intently at Mr. Newell. Ivan tensed. There was something familiar about the plain dark coat, the badly cut hair, the slightly sinister air of the man.

Mr. Newell nodded pleasantly, sizing up the man and pulling from his pocket a small notebook.

The man looked sharply at the notebook.

'Why have you brought out a notebook?'

'I like to write things down,' Mr. Newell said simply.

'There is no need to write anything down.' The man's voice was stern. 'You are a foreigner, I think.'

'That's right.' Mr. Newell smiled. 'And you are a policeman.'

The man bristled. 'Not at all. I am a librarian.' The man signaled a waitress for tea which was brought, to Ivan's surprise, immediately. 'And what are you doing in our Moscow? A tourist, perhaps?'

'Not at all. I am working here. May I ask your name?'

The man shifted uncomfortably, and with a false heartiness extended his hand. 'I am Viktor Nikolayev. And you?'

Ivan felt proud of the way Mr. Newell was talking to the stranger. Carefully he wrote on his pad 'Viktor Nikolayev.'

The man looked displeased. 'I think it is unusual that you write down my name. Why should you do this?'

'I like to remember names. You may write mine down. It is Robert Newell.'

'And your work?'

'I am a journalist.'

'And you, young Comrade.' The man turned a hooded gaze to Ivan. 'You are interested in journalism? You like to make friends with foreign journalists?'

Before Ivan could answer, Mr. Newell cut in. 'Obviously, being at the Planetarium, we…' with a sweep of his hand he included Ivan and himself… 'are interested in astronomy. It is a wonderful science, don't you agree? And the Soviet Union has done some exceptional work in this field.'

'Certainly. Of course. I believe Soviet science leads the world in this field.'

Mr. Newell did not disagree. He stood up with a friendly smile. 'I think we must make the best use of our time here.'

Ivan, too, stood quickly with a polite smile to the stranger.

'It was interesting to talk to you, Viktor Nikolayev.' Mr. Newell said the man's name distinctly. 'I hope you enjoy the Planetarium.'

Ivan and Mr. Newell left the man gazing unpleasantly after them.

'Have you seen that man before?' Mr. Newell asked quietly when they were out of earshot.

'No, I don't think so.' Ivan's knees felt a little shaky. 'Is he following you or me?'

Mr. Newell laughed softly. 'I don't know. Me, I expect. But it is a pretty sure thing neither of us will be neglected from now on, if the KGB can help it.'

'But why?' Ivan paused before a famous exhibit of moon rock brought back to the earth by the American astronauts.

'It could be only that I am a foreign journalist and they want to know who I am talking to. Perhaps it has something to do with Nyborg. I haven't been followed for awhile.'

'You don't think Mr. Nyborg is an informer?' Ivan gasped. 'He couldn't be!'

Mr. Newell gave Ivan a tolerant look. 'Surely you know by now not to trust anyone, Ivan. I don't know this Nyborg, and neither do you.'

Ivan had to nod in agreement.

'Then again, it might have something to do with your friend Volodia. Perhaps you were seen with him and he is being watched. Perhaps it's neither reason. We must always keep that in mind. I am working on many stories. This may have nothing to do with Alexander Ivanovich, the poet. But if it has, Nyborg informed.'

Ivan poked Mr. Newell softly. At the other end of the exhibit hall, Comrade Nikolayev was intently studying a large model of the solar system. Ivan and Mr. Newell laughed. But the tight feeling at the pit of Ivan's stomach did not go away.

The Watching Stranger

It had taken Ivan almost two long hours to get home from the Planetarium. A sudden hunch told him it would be a good precaution to set off in a direction opposite to his parents' apartment in case he was being followed. Then he could double back if the coast was clear.

Swept along by the weary crowds hurrying down the grand steps of Moscow subway, Ivan turned his head to glimpse a breathless Comrade Nikolayev rushing into the flow of people to pursue him.

With a grin and a violent plunge upward, Ivan pushed against the angered travellers and fought his way back to the top of the stairs. But he didn't smile a few minutes later as he eased himself into a seat on the first bus that had stopped outside the subway. Nikolayev, panting dreadfully, jumped onto the bus just as the doors were closing.

Ivan stared wide-eyed at the passing scene outside the bus windows, seeing only a blur. He had no idea where he was going. He felt utterly trapped. Glancing over his shoulder at Nikolayev several seats behind him, Ivan could see the smug expression of his face. He had Ivan where he wanted him. As soon as Ivan left the bus, Nikolayev would be close behind, obviously on a mission to find out where Ivan lived.

The bus wove its way through the evening rush hour traffic. Gradually people had to stand in the aisles, passing their kopecks forward to the woman collector who stood near the front calling out mechanical reminders to pay the fares, 'Comrades… Comrades.'

The aisles became packed with people, so many people that Ivan knew Nikolayev could no longer see him. Ivan knew Nikolayev would keep his eyes fixed on the door. How well he could see it, Ivan couldn't tell, but there was a chance that with the movement and push of people, Nikolayev would have difficulty keeping a clear view. Cautiously, Ivan eased out of his seat and hunched into the crowd. A woman with a string bag full of cabbages slipped quickly into his seat stepping on his toes without apology. Staying on the side of the aisle opposite Nikolayev and bending over as if he had a pain in his side, Ivan edged through the people toward the door. Not daring to stand too close to it, he waited. He was already past Nikolayev's seat and he knew the agent would have to turn his head to see the door.

The bus slowed down for a stop. A welcome gust of fresh air blew into the bus as the doors opened and a large group of school children pushed on. There was a slight groaning and shifting of the crowd. With a pang of guilt, Ivan plunged roughly through the last of the cluster of small boys and jumped off the bus just as the doors were wheezing shut, the edge of his coat barely escaping the closing doors. He had given Nikolayev the slip!

The tension he still felt made Ivan run through the streets, ignoring the disapproving stares of passers-by. He tried to figure out where he was in Moscow. Nothing was familiar. Ahead he saw another subway entrance and gratefully raced to it, down the stairs and onto the train platform. A gleaming train slid to a stop. It was going in Ivan's direction! Gratefully, Ivan pushed on, safely gliding away from Nikolayev at last.

With an anxious shake of her head, Momma cut the nourishing brow bread into heavy slices. Around the supper table, thick bowls of cabbage soup steamed invitingly. 'Ivan, you are getting more and more involved in something that is very dangerous.'

Poppa rubbed his forehead with concern. 'I have to agree with your Momma, Ivan. Any Soviet citizen who makes contact with a foreign journalist – well, that can mean nothing but trouble if it is discovered.'

'And we know it is discovered,' Katya added, trying to disguise her love of a good adventure by a worried frown.

Ivan pulled a face at Katya which she primly ignored. 'But he didn't succeed in finding out who I am or where I live, and I know Mr. Newell will never tell him.'

Poppa nodded. 'I thank the Lord for that, Ivan. That is a very great blessing. God's hand of protection was over you.'

Momma's face lit with a smile. 'Perhaps we could thank him for that and for the food before our soup gets cold.'

The family bowed. Ivan's heart was in prayer as Poppa praised God for preventing the agent from following Ivan home. A surge of love for God welled up in Ivan. How good a thing it was, he was thinking, to know that always, Christ was beside him. The amen of the grace pulled Ivan from his thoughts. He dipped his spoon hungrily into the soup.

'I wonder,' Poppa continued, 'if you have thought of the consequences of being followed, Ivan.'

'What consequences? Nikolayev doesn't know who I am.'

'But you must not contact Mr. Newell again. He will be watched and of course followed, and I cannot permit you to take such a risk. Next time you are seen with him, you will not get home without being stopped and questioned. The next time, there will be no chance for you to escape.'

Ivan was silent. He hadn't thought of this.

'And it's no use telephoning him,' Katya volunteered, her eyes sparkling. 'His telephone is sure to be bugged.'

'Katya, it's bad enough!' Ivan burst out. 'Momma, Katya thinks this is some kind of game.'

'I do not!' Katya shook her braids indignantly. 'And after all, who was it who found Mr. Newell, anyway?'

Ivan slumped a little in his chair with a groan.

'And if Ivan is questioned, why can't he just say that they made friends because Mr. Newell helped me when I got lost?' Katya persisted.

'We can say that,' Poppa rumpled her hair with a gentle hand. 'That explains how we met him, but it doesn't really explain why Ivan should keep on contacting him.'

'In any case,' Ivan declared firmly, 'I must see Volodia at the circus. Perhaps he will know something about all this. And I must tell him what Mr. Newell suspects about the Norwegian journalist.'

Momma gave Poppa a helpless look as she began collecting the empty soup bowls. When she sat down again, she began passing the generous bowl of Lobio that had been placed in the centre of the table. Ivan heaped the spicy red beans onto his plate and reached for another slice of bread. He noticed that with her eyes Momma was still urging Poppa to speak.

After Poppa had helped himself to the Lobio, he smiled at Ivan's tense face. 'I understand, son, that you want to help Volodia. I do not think you understand the seriousness of what is involved in the case of Volodia's uncle.'

Katya stirred uneasily in her chair. Even Katya was troubled by the gravity of Poppa's voice.

'We Christians in the Soviet Union sometimes do have troubles because we believe in God and try to follow what Jesus tells us to do. That is no surprise to you children.'

Ivan and Katya nodded. Poppa was talking so softly they had to listen intently to hear him.

'Sometimes we have to pay fines of a lot of money to the police for having Christian meetings in our homes. That is not allowed, is it?'

'No,' Ivan answered as quietly as Poppa was speaking.

'Sometimes pastors or church leaders are sent to prison camps because they distribute Bibles or teach Sunday school classes. That is not allowed, is it?'

This time Katya answered Poppa, leaving her chair and snuggling into his lap.

'And just as terrible, sometimes children are taken away from their parents because someone doesn't like it that they are learning too much about God and the Bible.'

Neither of the children answered Poppa. Both sighed heavily almost at the same time.

'But that is very unlikely to happen in Moscow,'

Momma added encouragingly. 'It is more likely to occur in small towns and villages, I think.'

'Yes, Momma,' Katya answered automatically, her mind still on Christian children who had to live in boarding school, away from their own homes and parents.

'But in all these problems and sufferings, there can be prayer to God and a Christian can be comforted and strengthened in knowing that Christ is with him.'

'Of course!' Ivan gave Poppa a steady smile. He knew Poppa didn't like to talk about these things.

'But sometimes, and perhaps more and more in our country, Christians who do not think the way the government wants them to think, or any other independent people…'

'Like Volodia's uncle…' Momma added softly.

Poppa nodded. '…who do not agree with the government, who criticise it, are put in hospitals for the insane. There, things can be done to their minds.' Poppa bit his lip thoughtfully, wondering how much more to say.

'What sort of things?' Katya demanded indignantly.

Poppa continued slowly. 'I don't know for sure. There are drugs that can be given to mix up a person's thinking. And other sorts of treatments may help people who really are insane. But…' his voice trailed off.

'But if a person is not insane, and these treatments are done to them, then it could hurt their minds?' Ivan ventured.

'Yes. So that then a Christian, for example, would no longer be in his right mind to be able to pray or to know that the Lord was with him.'

'It scares me,' Ivan said.

'It is a very fearful thing. A terrible thing to do. And of course our government does not want the rest of the world ever to know such things are really done.'

'And a poet in such sufferings could perhaps no longer write poetry,' Ivan expressed his thoughts aloud.

'Perhaps not. That is why Volodia is so determined to help his uncle. And why Mr. Newell is willing to risk his job as a journalist to help.'

'Our teachers say that the Soviet Union is the freest, most democratic country in the world,' Ivan said.

'Well,' Poppa answered, 'some people always think exactly what the government wants them to think. Some people never wonder if all they read in our newspapers is true. How could they know that innocent people are unjustly punished or cruelly locked up in hospitals for the insane?'

'You must not speak of these things to your friends at school,' Momma reminded the children. 'You would not be believed anyway. And it is certain you children would get into serious trouble for saying such things. Understand?'

'Of course, Momma. But Poppa, we can't leave Volodia to struggle alone for his uncle!'

There was a long silence in the room before Poppa answered. Ivan's heart lifted and Katya's eyes sparkled with relief when Poppa answered.

'No, we can't, Ivan. I am only saying, we must be very, very careful. And we must pray much.' Ivan nodded. There was another brief silence. As Katya slipped down from Poppa's lap, he pulled her back with a hug and a tickle. Katya began to laugh and Poppa continued to tickle until she shrieked and the whole family was laughing.

Outside their apartment building, a man, half hidden in a doorway, lit a cigarette and kept his eyes on the lighted windows of the Nazaroff apartment.

The Last Hope

The circus orchestra was rehearsing a comical tune to be played during a new act the clowns were creating. In the ring, Alexi, the animal trainer, exercised two of the horses, running easily beside them as they pranced in awkward playfulness to the music.

Volodia, swinging high above the scene, swooped in wide arcs from one trapeze to another with the freedom of a bird. He was practicing a difficult acrobatic turn, strapped into a safety harness which dangled him like a live puppet on a long rope secured to a centre point in the roof of the circus building.

'You're not concentrating again, Volodia!' Eugene, one of the troop's finest acrobats, called up to Volodia from the circus floor. 'We have all noticed lately. You're supposed to be practicing, not playing cosmonaut!'

Volodia waved in obedience, and with new determination swung out into the patter of twists and dives. He would have liked to ask Eugene to climb up and help him by catching him from the other trapeze, but his timing was not yet perfect. Until then, he knew he needed the security of the safety harness. He must put the worry of his uncle out of his mind. He had to get on with his work. It was essential to behave as if nothing were wrong.

If only Ivan would come! Had Ivan been able to contact Halvor Nyborg? And what would Ivan think of the document his uncle had given Volodia? What if Ivan didn't return? The fear stung his mind. Volodia twisted his body with force, as if to evade the thought itself. Eugene, still watching below, called up approvingly. 'Now you're getting it, Volodia! That was a good turn!'

Volodia grinned. Panting, he jumped on the aerial platform and released the trapeze. His hands were burning and a little damp. He shook some powder on them from a sac tied to the platform support and leaned back to rest a moment. He took some deep breaths. What if Ivan had decided it was all too dangerous? What if he didn't come back? Volodia shrugged. So who could blame him? It is not his problem! Something else would have to be done. It was a possibility that had to be faced.

With a fierce tug, Volodia yanked the rope dangling beside him that would swing the trapeze within his reach. With the sudden movement of the trapeze, Volodia's eye caught a movement on the circus floor. Eugene had gone, but from a doorway at the top of one of the ramps that led into the ring, someone was waving vigorously. Volodia's heart pounded with happiness. It was Ivan! With a joyful leap, Volodia caught the trapeze with both hands and let the dead weight of his body slow the trapeze down to a gentle motion above the centre ring. Then, grasping his support rope, he let go of the bar and lowered himself to the floor. In a second, he wiggled out of the support harness and raced to Ivan.

'It's about time!' Volodia was laughing and thumping Ivan on the back with delight. 'It's so good to see you, my friend!'

But Ivan's face was tight with tension.

'Volodia, can we go somewhere quickly? I'm not sure, but I may have been followed.'

Instantly Volodia pulled Ivan through the performers' exit, hurrying him across a long corridor and through another door marked 'Staff.' A short hallway later, they were safe inside a mirrored dressing room. Volodia locked the door and yanked together the drapes that hung at the window. The boys flung themselves into two easy chairs that were against the unmirrored wall of the room.

'Is it safe to talk?' Ivan whispered.

'I think so.' Volodia shrugged. 'Who can know?' Glancing at his radio on the dressing table, he switched it on. The news was being read dramatically from the Moscow studios. The boys relaxed. Even if the room were bugged, the radio voice would mask their conversation. Before sitting down again, Volodia dragged his chair against Ivan's.

'I've got to tell you–'

'The most amazing thing–'

Both boys had begun talking at once. They stopped abruptly in laughter.

'You go first, Ivan,' Volodia volunteered eagerly. 'Did you find Mr. Nyborg?'

'It was amazing. As you know, I had no idea where to start or how. But I heard about an American exhibit opening and that it was to be televised…'

'Oh, good!' Volodia couldn't restrain his approval.

'So Katya and I went. But it was so crowded and I couldn't get to the front where the newsmen were and Katya got lost and I had to spend all the time looking for her.'

Volodia's beaming face dimmed in confusion, but he didn't interrupt.

'I couldn't find her and finally had to go home. And there she was with a foreigner who brought her home.' Ivan paused dramatically.

'Not Nyborg?' Volodia raised his voice in astonishment.

Ivan shushed him with a cautious gesture. 'No! A Canadian. I didn't know what to do – if I should ask him to help me find Mr. Nyborg – if he could be trusted. I didn't say anything. Then I met him again and found out – I know it sounds impossible, Volodia – but he began to tell me he was a Christian.'

'A journalist? An educated man?' Volodia was incredulous.

Ivan laughed. 'There, you see, Volodia. It is not such a fairy story after all, is it? If a journalist…'

'But go on!' Volodia urged.

'Then I told him I also was a Christian and he could hardly believe that! A young person in atheist Russia! So, Volodia, I hope you will agree, but I knew I could trust him.'

Volodia thought for a moment. 'I think so, yes.'

'I asked him to help me find Mr. Nyborg, and Volodia, he did! Nyborg was actually leaving Moscow for the airport when Mr. Newell, the Canadian, got to his hotel. They had a brief talk and then he left. For Norway.'

Volodia groaned. 'He's gone! But he was our only hope.'

Ivan hesitated. 'I'm still not sure we can help your uncle. But Mr. Nyborg wasn't our hope.'

Volodia lifted his head and gazed at Ivan.

'It is God who is our hope,' Ivan grinned. 'And he hasn't gone anywhere.'

Volodia's voice reflected his discouragement. 'I

don't believe in God.'

'But I do!' Ivan grasped Volodia's arm in excitement. 'And God cares about you and your uncle whether you believe in him or not. That doesn't make any difference.'

Volodia looked startled. He shifted uneasily in his chair. 'You talk too much about God.'

'I'm sorry. But I must tell you about Mr. Newell. He is willing to try to help your uncle!'

A new light began to brighten Volodia's eyes, then was quickly dimmed. 'But why? He doesn't even know my uncle.'

Ivan laughed again. 'Why don't you shut your eyes, Volodia, and I'll say it fast! He wants to help your uncle because he is a Christian. Now let me tell you what has happened since.'

'But I must tell you something.' And as the woman newsreader's voice rose and fell, proudly announcing Soviet achievements on the international scene, Volodia told Ivan about his visit to his uncle and about the smuggled document. 'It is very dangerous for me to be hiding it,' Volodia concluded. 'I think you must take the document immediately, Ivan. I could be searched at any time because of my uncle.'

'But I am afraid I am being followed!' And Ivan told the story about his meeting with Mr. Newell at the Planetarium and then about his escape from the agent.

'Why should you be followed?' Volodia began pacing the room.

'Perhaps only because I was seen talking to a foreign journalist.'

'That could be. But then if you are followed, and followed here to me, the police will know we are trying to get publicity for my uncle through this Canadian. Then it may be worse for Uncle Sasha. Do you think you were followed here?'

'I don't know. When I left our apartment block, I thought a man who was standing outside our building began to follow me. He was very good, if he was following me. He stayed quite far behind. I tried to lose him. I went along a lot of small streets and turned in several directions and he seemed to stay behind me. But then, some woman stopped him and began talking to him and I turned a corner and ran!'

Volodia laughed.

'When I slowed down and began walking again, he was nowhere in sight, so perhaps he wasn't following me.'

'Or if he was, the woman stopped him long enough, so he doesn't know where you are now.'

'Right!'

'Then this is your chance to take away the document. Perhaps the next time, you will not be so lucky.'

Ivan was glad Volodia had stopped pacing. Now he was sitting on the wide sill of the window staring at Ivan's reflection in the mirrors.

'But you don't want to take the document? It is too dangerous?' Volodia asked politely. He knew what a calamity it would be for anyone to be found with such a paper – documentation that a healthy person was locked up with the insane.

'I couldn't take it home,' Ivan said slowly. 'That would be too risky. Our apartment could easily be searched just on the excuse that we are Christians.'

Volodia waited anxiously.

'Mr. Newell!' Ivan exclaimed. 'We want a journalist to give publicity to your uncle. Of course! This is the proof of what we are saying. Mr. Newell said he needed proof! I will take it to him.'

'That may not be so easy. How can you go to his house? Do you know where he lives?'

Ivan shook his head from side to side.

'Perhaps I could mail it to Mr. Nyborg. You could find out his address, Ivan. Perhaps someone in the circus who is traveling would mail it for me outside Russia.'

Ivan looked alarmed. 'Volodia, I don't think this is true, but there is something…'

'About Mr. Nyborg? He is my uncle's friend!'

'Mr. Newell told me that he began to be closely followed right after he met and talked to Mr. Nyborg about your uncle. That's why there was an agent watching us at the Planetarium.'

'I don't believe it!' Volodia jumped down from the window and began pacing. 'He is my uncle's best friend! My uncle has dedicated poems to him!'

Ivan looked helplessly at Volodia. Finally he spoke. 'Are you so positive, Volodia, so completely positive about Mr. Nyborg that you would mail him the document?'

Volodia stared angrily at Ivan for a moment. Then hot tears flashed in his eyes. 'You take the document,' he said. 'I have heard it said, and not just once, either, that in our country only Christians can be trusted.' Volodia's voice broke. Once Mr. Nyborg had been his great hope. Now he had only the Christians and God.

Hard Work

Ivan knew it was stupid to run, but he couldn't help it. The document zipped inside his jacket thumped against his chest as he rushed through the late Sunday morning streets. People out for a pleasant stroll in the early spring sunshine frowned at Ivan's disruption of the quiet morning mood.

Finally, at the end of a long street, Ivan saw the branch post office to which he was running. There would be a public telephone. Panting, he stumbled up the steps and into the building. The telephone was not in use! Pulling a small coin out of his pocket, he dialed Mr. Newell's number. His heart was pounding from running and from suspense. Mr. Newell had to be home. But it was Sunday! He might well be in church! Ivan was so tense he almost did not hear a the faint voice at the other end of the line as he was hanging up the phone. With a jerk, he pulled the phone back to his ear.

'Mr. Newell?'

'Yes,' the voice didn't sound like Mr. Newell. A stab of fear shot through Ivan.

'It doesn't sound like you,' he said doubtfully.

There was a thick laugh. 'I have a rather bad cold, I'm afraid.'

'This is me,' Ivan said cautiously.

There was a slight pause. 'Oh, yes, I understand,' Mr. Newell replied.

'Do you know who I am?' Ivan persisted.

'Yes. Christ is risen!'

Ivan relaxed joyfully as he gave the ancient Russian response:

'He is risen indeed!' No KGB agent would know that greeting, or think to say it.

'I need to see you,' Ivan said carefully.

'Yes, of course.' There was a longer pause. Ivan knew Mr. Newell would be thinking. If his phone were bugged, he would have to answer with extreme caution.

'You know where our mutual friend works?'

'The Moscow circus,' Ivan answered quickly, 'Yes.'

'There is a square, toward the Kremlin.'

Ivan thought hard. Mr. Newell couldn't mean Commune Square. That was beyond the circus away from the centre of the city.

'There's only one right there,' Mr. Newell prompted.

Of course! Trubnaya Square. 'I know it!' Ivan exclaimed.

'I'll come as soon as I can. Wait for me there.'

'Thank you. Goodbye.'

An impatient woman pulled the telephone receiver from Ivan and pushed him aside. But Ivan was so relieved he didn't mind. Sauntering in the spring sunshine, he began to enjoy the mild air and the pale rays of the sun. Soon all the ice on the river would be melted and the pleasure boats and barges would begin their journeys. Tourists from all over the world would come to admire the beautiful churches of the Kremlin, to visit Lenin's tomb, and the face of Moscow would brighten and become alive.

There were many babushkas in the square, watching over tiny children still bundled against a possible chill. The old grandmothers sat in twos and threes on benches, occasionally chatting with each other, their eyes as quick as a bird's to any movement of the children playing nearby.

Ivan smiled at them. He knew many were Christians. They would have been children themselves at the time of the Revolution, yet they managed to find God in lifetimes that had seen civil war in Russia, and world war. Their lives had been difficult, yet in spite of sufferings and the constant teaching of government that there is no God, they became firm believers. 'Those faithful old women, they are our glory,' Momma once told Ivan.

'They also do a good deal of teaching about God,' Poppa had added. 'Even when the mothers and fathers of the little children do not believe in God, the grandmothers see to it, when they can, that the children are taught about God and to pray and learn Bible stories. They aren't afraid of anybody!'

Ivan's eyes swept over the huge square looking for Mr. Newell. Of course, if Mr. Newell thought he was being followed, he would have to shake off the KGB man before coming to the square. It might take him a long time.

'Would you like an ice cream?' said a voice behind Ivan.

Ivan wheeled around in surprise. 'You are so quick!'

Mr. Newell handed Ivan a vanilla ice cream as he answered with a laugh, 'There was no one watching our apartment. Then I realised; the police know my actions so well, they knew I would go to church on

Sunday morning. No doubt there is someone at the Moscow Church or the English chapel looking for me. And I was home with a cold.'

Ivan laughed and bit into the ice cream gratefully. 'Thank you. This is good.'

They began walking toward a less central part of the square.

'How is your friend?' Mr. Newell asked.

'He's all right. I went to see him. That's why I called you.'

'What's up?'

'He was permitted to visit his uncle. For purposes of persuasion. He was supposed to convince his uncle to cooperate with the doctors and admit he needed treatment.'

'But it was a good chance to see him!'

Ivan nodded in agreement.

'I suppose there was an attendant with him all the time?'

Mr. Newell smiled in enjoyment at Ivan's account of how the uncle had outwitted the doctor by having another patient create a disturbance and draw away the doctor's attention. But his face grew alive with interest as Ivan told him about the document.

'Ivan, that's wonderful. That would be some sort of proof if the document really contains what you say!' Mr. Newell interrupted Ivan's account in his excitement. 'Have you seen the document?'

'Actually, I have it. Inside my jacket.'

Even Mr. Newell looked around nervously.

'We want you to take it. If you are willing.' Ivan said hopefully.

'Ivan, that's the best possible thing to do. I can't be searched – or my apartment – nearly as easily as you Russians can, so the document would be far safer with me. And I will be able to use it for a story – which is what Volodia wants.'

'Exactly,' Ivan agreed. 'But how can I give it to you? Even in the square there is likely to be someone watching people. And you are a foreigner.'

'We'll have to do this quickly.' Mr. Newell unzipped his jacket part of the way. 'In a few minutes I will stop and bend over to tie my shoe. When I do, you stand in front of me as I am bending over. Take the document out of your jacket and as fast as you can, slip it into the top part of mine. When I stand up, I'll zip up my jacket. The document won't fall out because of the elastic around the bottom. Ready?'

'Ready.'

Mr. Newell casually stooped to tie his shoe. In a flash, Ivan pulled the document from his jacket and stuffed it inside Mr. Newell's. His hands shook and a bit of the paper was snagged on the zipper, but in spite of Ivan's difficulty, Mr. Newell continued to tie his shoe as if nothing were happening. When he straightened up, he pulled the zipper to the top and shoved his hands into the jacket pockets. They resumed their walk at a slow pace.

'Now what?' Ivan asked.

'As much as I don't like to say it, probably the best thing is for you and me not to contact each other for a while. If I need to see you, I'll send you a postcard in the mail. I have some from the monastery at Zagorsk. The postcard will mean to meet again in this square. Under the stamp I'll put the day and the time. Is that all right'

'Yes.' Ivan was thoughtful. 'Then there's nothing else I can do? Or Volodia?'

'Nothing else Volodia can do. But you, Ivan, you can do some hard work.'

'What? I'd really like to be able to do something. Anything you think.'

Mr. Newell's voice was gentle but intense.

'Pray Ivan! Every day for as long as you can.'

Ivan nodded.

Smiling, Mr. Newell embraced Ivan in the Russian way and hurried out of the square.

Ivan trailed listlessly out of the park. He felt somehow let down. It was much easier to do something than to pray. It was curious that Mr. Newell called prayer 'hard work.' Yet it was very hard to make oneself pray for a long time. It was hard work. Noble work, too. With new resolve Ivan squared his shoulders toward home. Momma and Poppa would be getting back from church and Katya would have the borscht hot. After lunch, Ivan would pray.

A Sudden Shock

Ivan was in a peaceful mood as he climbed the stairs to his apartment. It was a good feeling to think of spending Sunday afternoon in prayer for Volodia and his uncle, for Mr. Newell and the story he would be writing, for the Christians in the West who would read it. He pulled open the door of the apartment with a smile, ready to tell Momma and Poppa and Katya how the Lord was working.

The scene that met his eyes made him freeze in the doorway. Momma was weeping in the big chair by the sofa. Poppa was pacing up and down and shaking his head and arguing with a man Ivan had never seen before. Ivan stared at Momma in distress. Seldom had he seen Momma cry.

'Shut the door, Ivan!' Poppa ordered in an abrupt voice. Ivan automatically closed the door, still staring in confusion at the sight.

The stranger took a few steps toward Ivan. 'This is your son, Ivan Sergeivich,' he stated.

Poppa strode to Ivan and put an arm loosely around his shoulder. 'It is. He has been for a walk. I suppose that is not forbidden for children on a Sunday morning?'

Momma blew her nose and looked in alarm at Poppa. 'Sergei,' she said softly, almost in a warning voice.

'It is permitted,' the man replied pleasantly.

It was not good when the police were pleasant, Ivan knew. That meant they felt secure about whatever charges they were making.

Poppa drew Ivan to the sofa and they both sat down. 'I must insist on being told the whereabouts of my daughter,' Poppa said in a way that showed Ivan he had already asked many times before.

'Certainly. There is no problem. There are only some questions I must require you to answer.'

'Then take me to Katya and I will answer them,' Poppa said quietly. 'Whatever you wish to know, I will be able to be of more help if I am not so worried about my little girl. I go to church and come home, and instead of finding my children, I am told that my daughter has been taken for interrogation.'

'It was not the intention of the authorities to frighten either you or your daughter,' the man replied in a smooth voice that Ivan disliked. 'Of course, we expected your family would be together and the few questions could be answered quickly.'

'Then why did you take her?' Poppa demanded. 'Why could you not wait here?'

The man shrugged. 'It was my superior's decision. It was the intention to question your family at the police station and he intended to pick you up at the church. If he missed you, I was to stay and bring you if you returned home.'

'Then take us!' Poppa said in exasperation.

'Your daughter is in good hands. She is not frightened at all. I do not understand why you are making such a fuss.'

Ivan thought of Katya, alone in an interrogation room at some police office. Indignation rose in him. Momma put a hand on his arm.

'The few questions…' The man took out a small notebook and pencil. 'They concern your friendship with one so-called Robert Newell, supposedly a Canadian journalist.'

Ivan's stomach lurched. Poppa bit his lip. It was a game he knew he was losing. Until he answered the questions, he would not see Katya. Perhaps even then, there would be further delays. Yet it was not possible to force the police.

'How is it that an ordinary Russian family, a factory worker, would wish to make contact with a foreign newsman?'

The policeman looked with a blank face at Poppa. Momma had stopped weeping, but Ivan's stomach was so knotted that he was glad the question was not directed at him. He wasn't sure that he would be able to answer calmly.

'My daughter and son went to see the American exhibit a few weeks ago. In the crowd, our daughter got lost and this foreigner brought her home. Apparently he knows Moscow well enough that he was able to find the correct bus and in the friendly way of Canadians, he brought her to our door.'

'We gave him tea to thank him for his kindness, that is all,' Momma spoke quietly. Ivan was proud of the steadiness of her voice. He knew she was terribly worried about Katya.

'Canadians are more friendly than Russians then?' The pencil poised in midair.

'Of course not. It just happened that way.'

'And no Russian at the exhibit was able to help a lost child?'

Poppa took a deep breath. 'I am sure anyone there would have helped her. Surely it is not reasonable to be suspicious just because it happened that a foreigner helped her.'

'You attend the Moscow Baptist Church?'

Poppa nodded in agreement. 'All this is already on your records. If we could go to my daughter where she is detained, I am sure you could check all this.'

'And this so-called Mr. Newell attends the English-speaking Christian chapel in Moscow?'

'I have no idea,' Poppa said, surprised. 'He certainly made no mention of it to us. We had no reason to discuss religion.'

'You did not discuss religion with this man?' The policeman gave Poppa and then Momma a sharp look.

Momma shook her head vehemently. 'Not at all. Not in the slightest way,' Poppa asserted.

The policeman shook his head. 'It is very strange, isn't it? Certainly an odd coincidence.' The policeman wrote something in his book. 'And your did not discuss religion with him when he was bringing her home?'

'Perhaps we ought to ask my daughter. I do now know. I would like to know from her. I am, however, almost certain that the subject did not come up.'

'I'm sure not!' Ivan exclaimed impulsively. 'Mr. Newell was very surprised when he found out we were believers.'

As soon as the words were out of his mouth, Ivan's whole body went hot. Poppa didn't even look at Ivan, but closed his eyes an instant as if he'd been hit.

The policeman smiled at Ivan. 'And when did he find out.'

Ivan's mind was whirling. He couldn't think. He knew everything depended on his answer, depended on a natural-sounding answer, and still a truthful one.'

Momma suddenly stood up. 'I am sorry, comrade officer. You will understand as a mother, it has been distressing to me to come home and find my daughter gone. I feel quite ill. If we are not to go immediately to the station, is it possible that I might make some tea? I am feeling quite ill.'

'I'm sure the police will permit a mother to have a cup of tea,' Poppa said to the officer.

The man flushed in irritation. 'I do not have time to wait for such things. This is not a social visit.'

'But you are not questioning my wife,' Poppa said encouragingly. 'She is a mother, with a mother's heart. I think nothing will be slowed down if she merely makes a cup of tea. Unless, of course, you will be taking us immediately to our little girl.'

The policeman gave in ungraciously with a wave of dismissal to Momma. Ivan flashed her a grateful look as she got up.

The policeman turned again to Ivan. 'You were telling me when this Mr. Newell found out you were a Christian family.'

By this time Ivan had recovered his composure. 'I believe I happened to tell him,' he said easily. The policeman took Momma's place on the couch beside Ivan. 'It so happened he was telling me about life in Ottawa and about Canada. He said perhaps I would find it hard to understand, but that many people in Canada believe in God and go to church.' Ivan looked with some satisfaction at the discomfort of the policeman.

'Religion is dying out in the West,' the officer said automatically.

Ivan ignored the statement. 'I told him I did understand about believing in God because I also believe in God. He was very surprised.'

'I was not aware of this conversation,' Poppa said uneasily.

'Then when did it take place?' The officer looked hard at Ivan.

'My son walked our guest to the bus stop after he left our apartment,' Poppa replied quickly. 'It seemed only polite after he had traveled so far to bring Katya home.'

'He told me about the Canadian hockey team, the Maple Leafs,' Ivan volunteered. 'Of course, they are not so good as our Russian team. I believe we have defeated them in international competition.'

'Of course we have defeated them! We always defeat them!' the policeman replied hotly.

Momma returned from the kitchen with a sweet smile to the policeman. 'Are we going now to our daughter?'

The policeman looked helplessly around the apartment.

'You are welcome to search our apartment. There is nothing you will find, but we would be happy for you to search,' Poppa offered.

The man hesitated. 'We are just getting into all of this,' he said. 'We have not gotten yet to the bottom of it all.'

'We are glad to answer your questions,' Poppa replied, standing up.

'Get your coats, then,' the officer said abruptly. 'We will continue this interrogation at the police station.'

Interrogation

The police station was not far from the Nazaroff apartment. Ivan could see Poppa and Momma were relieved that they did not have a long car ride to find Katya. Somehow the fact that the interrogation was taking place nearby was reassuring.

Ivan had expected Katya's eyes to be red from weeping. Instead, Katya flashed Ivan a fleeting, defiant grin and a satisfied lift of her chin as they entered the room. Momma greeted Katya calmly and Poppa gave her a brief hug.

So Katya is pleased with herself, Ivan was thinking. She is pretty sure she hasn't told anything about Volodia.

Katya's eyes widened as she fixed an innocent look on Poppa. 'I am sorry to have caused any problem, Poppa, by letting the foreigner bring me home. I didn't know it would make trouble!'

Poppa gave Katya just the slightest skeptical look. 'Don't overdo it,' he seemed to be saying.

But Katya was enjoying the limelight. Ivan felt uncomfortable. 'I would have just told him that one of our good Russian babushkas could bring me home, if I had thought that there was anything wrong.'

The policeman shifted his weight irritably and directed his question at Katya. 'When did you first know that this so-called Mr. Newell was a Christian believer as you are?'

Katya was thrown completely off balance. All her innocent assurance melted away and left a look of stupefied astonishment. 'When…Ivan told me…' she stammered.

There was silence in the room. The officer continued to wait. 'The whole truth,' he said threateningly.

'…after…they met and talked…' Katya broke off the sentence in fear.

'The parents will wait outside,' the officer stated. Quickly he moved to the door and pushed Momma and Poppa outside. The door shut with a metallic click. Ivan knew they were locked in.

'And when did your brother meet and 'talk' to this Western journalist?' The policeman sat down behind the desk in the room and idly pulled out a file. He flipped it open and made a brief notation.

'I…I don't remember…'

'I think you do. It is best if you cooperate from the very beginning. Otherwise you will keep your parents waiting a long time.'

'It was about a month ago,' Ivan said. 'I am interested in life in Canada and Mr. Newell said he wanted to more about life in Moscow. He has a nephew in Canada about my age and…'

'How did you get in touch with him again?'

'I telephoned him.'

'How did you know his number?'

'He gave it to our family when he brought Katya back.'

'Why?'

'I don't know. I think it is a friendly custom. I don't know.'

'And you wanted to tell him stories about how it

is to be a Christian in Russia, eh? And so you called him and arranged to have a walk.'

'No!' Ivan retorted with conviction. 'I didn't even know he was a Christian when I called him. He told me on the walk.'

'Of course.' The officer was writing furiously on a piece of paper in the file. Ivan wondered what could have been important in what he said. 'But he asked you questions about your religious life?'

'No,' Ivan replied with conviction. He was remembering how they had talked about Volodia's uncle.

'You were seen with him at the Moscow Planetarium. You told me you went on a walk.'

How much did the KGB know? For the first time, Ivan began to feel uneasy. 'Well, we went to the Planetarium, obviously.'

'Was this another time? Or the time you referred to as a 'walk'?'

'Why are you asking these questions?' Ivan demanded. 'Is there a criminal charge that you are bringing against me for making friends with a foreigner? I do not understand why I am being asked all these questions. I would like my parents to explain to me what it is that I have done wrong.'

'No one says you have done anything wrong.'

'Then why am I here being asked questions?'

'Perhaps the journalist has done something wrong,' the officer answered slyly. 'Perhaps you can be of assistance to the Soviet State.'

Ivan began to be frightened. Had Mr. Newell had time to write the articles? Could he have distributed them so quickly? Of course not! Ivan had just given the document to him today. The documents could not have been discovered so quickly either. Ivan took a deep breath. 'I am glad to be of assistance to my country.'

'These meetings with Mr. Newell. What was the purpose?'

'I had never met a Canadian before.'

'Me either!' Katya exclaimed helpfully. 'Canada is much like Russia – only not, of course, as progressive as our country.'

'You might be interested to know your journalist friend has been detained. He is in the next room.'

Katya looked alarmed. Ivan gazed at the officer. Surely he was not telling the truth. Ivan had just left Mr. Newell. But he could have been picked up immediately. Then the document would have been found! Ivan's mouth went dry.

'Yes, we have had him here for several hours. Since last night. There is nothing we do not know. You had better tell everything you know.'

Ivan relaxed. He wanted to laugh. The officer bent for a moment to reach a pack of cigarettes in the bottom desk drawer. With the slightest movement of his head, Ivan signalled 'no' to Katya. She too lost the look of fear.

The flame of a match flared for an instant as the officer inhaled. 'Well?'

'Mr. Newell has not discussed his newspaper work with me,' Ivan offered. 'I don't really even know what he is doing in Moscow. Why is he detained?'

'That is the business of the police. But it is a serious matter to have a friend who is a criminal.'

'But he hasn't been brought to trial yet, has he?' Katya asked sweetly. 'So it is possible he is not guilty.'

'It is possible, certainly. But we never make mistakes.' There was silence in the room. Finally the officer said, 'Are you certain there is nothing you can tell me that would be of use to Soviet justice?'

'I assure you with all my heart, there is nothing more at all I can tell you that would serve Soviet justice!' Ivan answered sincerely.

The officer shrugged as he unlocked the door. To the surprise of the children, Momma and Poppa were waiting on a bench in the hall outside of the interrogation room.

'You may go!' the officer announced. Then, looking severely at Ivan, he added, 'You are all to report any further contacts with this man.'

Katya raised innocent eyes to the officer. 'But he is detained. How will we have contacts with him any more?'

Ivan could have poked Katya. Sometimes she really did push things too far. One could never be sure what the police would do if embarrassed.

The officer looked blank, then flushed slightly. 'If it is determined that detainment is unnecessary, then he will be released, obviously.'

'Yes, obviously,' Ivan agreed, this time really poking Katya.

'Come on, children,' Poppa said, turning to the door. 'Your mother is tired and ready for an afternoon rest.'

Katya gave a shy smile to the officer.

'Goodbye, Comrade. I too will be glad to aid Soviet justice.'

The officer stared at Katya briefly. With a yank, Ivan pulled her out of the door. 'You think you're so funny, Katya!' Ivan muttered. 'This is nothing to joke about!' Before Katya could open her mouth to protest, he added, 'And you aren't even involved in all this!'

Katya gave Ivan a mischievous smile. 'You just might be surprised, Ivan!'

Katya's Courage

Volodia hunched at the side of Ivan's apartment building, shivering in the early spring cold. He moved his weight slightly and almost put his foot down on a tender yellow crocus that was just pushing up from the hard earth. Shaking his head in exasperation, he moved again, just in time to see Katya hurrying out of the building. 'Over here!'

Katya's brown eyes flashed with alertness. In a moment she was with Volodia, half-hidden in the corner of the building. 'Ivan would kill me if he knew!' she whispered happily.

Volodia grinned. 'He'd kill me too! But there's no other way. He's being watched.'

'So are you!' Katya peered about anxiously.

'He's taken so many risks for my uncle. There's no one but you. Are you sure you're not afraid?'

Katya was quiet for a moment. 'I have been praying about all this, Volodia. I want you to know I have prayed much for the escape of your uncle.'

Volodia nodded, not quite as quickly as once he would have. His answer was quiet. 'At first I put all my hopes on Mr. Nyborg, the Norwegian journalist. I was angry that it turned out that all I had to depend on were Christians.' He gave Katya a gentle look. 'Now I am glad. Perhaps it isn't a bad idea to pray.'

Katya smiled. 'You'll see what God can do. I would be too scared for this if it weren't for God.'

'Then I am glad for your faith in God, if it makes you brave.'

'Not 'it', Volodia, Him. God makes me brave.'

'All right!' Volodia shook his head impatiently. 'Do you remember everything you are to do?'

'Yes.'

'You will go to visit a patient named Mr. Orlov. He is harmless but truly insane and my uncle says he talks all the time about missing his daughter. He will be glad to see you. I hope you don't mind that I had to say I knew your family and that they were once neighbours with him and that you and he had a friendship – that you will come to bring him some crocuses.'

Katya shrugged. 'I don't mind. But you shouldn't lie, Volodia.'

Volodia ignored the reproof. 'He is so harmless, he even works around the hospital. With his help, my uncle got the key. It's a great pity my uncle couldn't just keep the key and unlock the door himself. His eyesight has been affected by the insulin treatments they have given him. He is almost sure he couldn't see the lock clearly enough to use the key.'

'Oh, Volodia!'

'His eyesight always has been poor, but now it's much worse.'

'How did your uncle get Mr. Orlov to give him the key?'

'He likes my uncle because Uncle reads poetry to him. And Uncle said he could arrange a visit from his little girl.'

'How did your uncle know about me?'

'I told him all about your family the last time I visited him. The whole plot was figured out by my uncle. But let's get back to the plan.'

'I will go and visit this man…'

'Mr. Orlov.'

'Yes, after school today, taking the crocuses. When I am to leave the hospital, I will go out of the ward and instead of going to the front door, turn right at the first hall along the corridor.'

'Yes, and you'll have to do it fast.'

'There is a door at the dead end of the hall that leads out to an incinerator where garbage is burned. I unlock the door and then get back to the main hall and leave.'

'Everything depends on how quickly you do it. My uncle says no one goes along that hall except workers to burn garbage and they don't do that in visiting hours. It is unlikely that you will meet anyone, but if you do…'

'I'll just ask the way to the front door.'

'Yes. But if you don't get the door unlocked, all will be lost because we have only this one chance. Uncle says his eyesight…'

'I have been praying…'

Volodia nodded impatiently. 'Here is the key.' Volodia pressed the cold metal into Katya's hand. Suddenly Katya felt scared.

'Where will your uncle go when he escapes? How will he hide?'

Volodia's face seemed to close. 'I cannot tell you that.'

Katya nodded quickly. 'Of course.' Another thought distressed her. 'But what about the key? Won't they know at the hospital that the key is missing?'

Volodia laughed. 'They do know. Mr. Orlov said it fell into the garbage and was thrown into the incinerator. My uncle said everyone was angry at poor Mr. Orlov, but he didn't notice. And there was nothing they could do.'

A prowling cat rustled the bushes along the side of the apartment. Volodia and Katya both jumped.

'I have to go!' Volodia gave Katya an intense look. 'Good luck, Katya!'

Katya opened her moth to tell Volodia that there was no such thing as luck, but then closed it again. 'God go with you, Volodia!' she said with a determined smile.

Lots of people were in the reception hall of the Serbsky Institute. Katya felt very small under the high ceilings of the room. Her heart was pounding almost in rhythm with her steps as she approached the desk. Several irritable clerks were directing people to visiting areas.

The brittle cellophane wrapping of the crocus plant she was carrying rustled against her jacket and pricked her chin. Katya kept both hands around the plant to restrain herself from checking the key in her pocket. Before she spoke, she cleared her throat.

A woman with short straight hair cut evenly all around her head glared at Katya suspiciously.

'Who are you here for?' she demanded.

'I've come to visit Mr. Orlov – Georgi Orlov. He's allowed to have visitors.'

The woman flipped through an index and then stared again at Katya. 'Who are you? You aren't a relative?'

Katya smiled sweetly. 'I only came to bring him this plant. He thinks I am his daughter, but I'm really no relative at all, as you say. I'll only stay to give him the spring flowers. Our teacher says our country is built upon friendship and one helping the other. I thought the plant might help him not feel alone.'

'Ward five is along to the left corridor and at the top of the stairs. You aren't to hang about. I want you out in fifteen minutes.'

'Thank you, Comrade.' Katya walked as correctly as she could to the hallway. She had felt calm enough talking to the clerk, but now inside the actual hospital, she felt nervous. What would crazy people be like? Perhaps someone would jump out of a corner and strangle her! Perhaps she would have to see someone who looked horrible or who screamed and raved.

Katya moved her eyes to catch a glimpse of the wards she was passing. White iron beds. People resting or moving slowly about. Patients sitting in straight chairs. Visitors chatting or comforting patients. From a corner of a room someone laughed suddenly and Katya jumped. But it was a visitor, embracing an old grandmother.

The doors of ward five were open wide and Katya entered hesitantly. Immediately a nurse came to her side.

'Mr. Orlov, please.' Katya smiled and tried to keep her voice as business-like as possible. 'He's allowed visitors. I've brought him a crocus and I will only stay a minute. The clerk at the desk said it was all right.'

The nurse walked briskly to a bed on the far side of the room. Katya was ablaze with curiosity. Which of the patients staring at her was Volodia's uncle? None of them looked to Katya like poets.

'Comrade!' the nurse said sharply to an elderly gentleman lying on his bed.

The old man sat up in bewilderment. When he

saw Katya, his faded face flushed with pleasure. 'Valentina!' he exclaimed.

Katya accepted his rapturous hug awkwardly. The nurse sighed impatiently and moved back to the door.

'I brought you some crocuses,' Katya said shyly.

'I knew you would come!' The old man's eyes never left Katya's face. 'You look exactly the same. Only bigger, of course. You are a big girl now.'

'Yes,' Katya said. She could feel her eyes stinging with tears.

'You mustn't cry!' The old man was laughing quietly in pleasure. 'I knew you would come when you could. Is your mother well?'

'Oh, yes.' Katya held out the plant to Mr. Orlov. Absently he took it and put it on his bed.

'And Peter is still in the Army? And Sasha, did he pass his examinations? And did we get the Baderenkos' apartment? We were the first to ask for it. They should have given it to us long ago, you know.'

'Yes, I'm sure.' Panic was fluttering inside Katya's chest. There was so little time.

The old man was holding on to Katya's hand so hard it hurt. 'Sasha shouldn't worry so much about his examinations. You must tell him not to worry. He must think of his health.' The old man's voice fell to a whisper. 'There are ways of helping him. You must tell him I have ways of helping him. Contacts.'

Katya nodded.

'And I have been planning for your future. You need a long rest this summer. I will take you to our dachau outside of Moscow. A long rest, lots of sunshine, and picking berries. We will pick berries. And when it is time for school, the best school.' The old man looked anxious. 'You wouldn't mind going to the best school?'

The lump in her throat was choking Katya. She shook her head. The man looked very pleased. 'They say you are all grown up! They try to fool me and confuse me. And look at you! Of course you are a big girl. But not grown up yet. Of course not. I knew you would come!'

The nurse stood beside Katya. 'This girl must go now. She only came to bring you the crocuses.'

Joy filled the old man's eyes. 'This is my daughter,' he said in a trembling voice. 'She has come at last!'

The nurse was pulling Katya's hand away from the old man. 'That's enough!' she ordered. 'Lie down now.'

The old man touched Katya's arm. 'Valentina! You don't have to go yet!'

Impulsively Katya threw her arms around the old man. 'I am glad I could come!'

'You will come back?' The old man's plea followed Katya across the ward.

Katya nodded her head vigorously without looking back. Tears stood in her eyes. 'I will bring my Momma next time if I can.'

In the hall she leaned against the wall and wiped her eyes. She had almost forgotten the key.

Smuggled In

There was a rough knock at the door. Ivan put down his history book and rose from the couch to answer it. It was a neighbor, Comrade Bukovsky from the large first floor apartment in the building. Although he was only a minor official in the government, he had managed to get a telephone. His wife was an invalid and many times Momma had brought her food or stayed with her when her illness got worse. Comrade Bukovsky had principles against making friends with religious people, but all the same he was grateful to Momma and had offered his telephone number for the Nazaroffs to give out or use in emergency.

Bukovsky had sleeves rolled up and was holding a small glass of vodka. He looked unhappy about being disturbed from his evening pleasures, but all the same he managed a nod of greeting to Ivan. 'I don't know what could be so important, Ivan Sergeivich,' he announced. 'There is a woman on my telephone asking to speak to you.'

'To me?' Ivan was truly astonished.

'Come along then!' Bukovsky turned and made his way to the stairs. 'She's been waiting long enough,' he threw over his shoulder.

'My parents are out shopping,' Ivan called foolishly to the man.

Bukovsky paused at the top of the stairs, shaking

his head at Ivan's stupidity. 'She wants to talk to you. I certainly hope, Comrade, this is an emergency!'

Ivan pulled the apartment door closed after him and hurried to the stairs. Inside Bukovsky's apartment was the smell of sausages and vodka and a faint hospital-like smell from Mrs. Bukovsky's room. The telephone was on top of a small piano in the living room, surrounded by tiny glass figurines of horses and chickens and sea creatures. Ivan lifted the telephone receiver carefully from the multitude of glass animals that surrounded it on the piano top.

'Is this Ivan Nazaroff?' The woman's voice had a cultured Moscow accent. 'One moment, please.'

'Ivan?' Mr. Newell's voice seemed to boom into the living room.

Ivan glanced nervously at Comrade Bukovsky who was sipping his vodka and pretending to read the day's Pravda. His eyes caught Ivan's over the top of the newspaper, then disappeared. Ivan's heart lurched. Mr. Newell spoke Russian with a thick Western accent. Would Mr. Bukovsky be able to hear?

'It is urgent, Ivan. Are you alone in the room?'

'No,' Ivan answered brightly.

'Can you meet me as soon as possible at the same place?'

An image of Trubnaya Square flashed into Ivan's mind. 'Yes.'

'Good.' There was a slight pause. 'Will you need to tell your neighbor what the emergency is?'

'I think so.' Ivan felt Mr. Bukovsky's eyes on him.

'Ivan, Katya is with me. She's been hurt.'

'Hurt?' Ivan blurted out in alarm.

'It's not serious. Tell your neighbor she fell,

running down the subway steps. It's not serious, Ivan,' Mr. Newell repeated.

'My parents are out shopping,' Ivan volunteered.

'Just come, Ivan. There's no need to worry them about Katya. Goodbye.'

At the click of the receiver, Comrade Bukovsky stood up. 'Someone is hurt?'

Ivan smiled slightly in reassurance. 'It's nothing serious. Katya fell running to the subway. She just needs some help home.'

Comrade Bukovsky nodded understandingly as he opened his door. 'I'm sorry to hear it.' He took another sip of vodka. 'But she's all right?'

'Oh, yes,' Ivan assured him.

Bukovsky closed the door contentedly. He had been a good neighbor.

Ivan's mind was in a turmoil as he raced through the darkening streets to the square. He had known something mysterious was going on! Katya had not waited for him after school and was not home when he arrived. He had wondered if she had gone shopping with Momma and Poppa. But Katya hated lines and he had thought it unlikely. And there was more to the call than Katya's being hurt! If that were all, Mr. Newell would have seen to it that she was brought home. And what was Katya doing with Mr. Newell?

At the square Ivan stopped against a tree, gasping for breath and trying to make out the figures of Katya and Mr. Newell among the few people hurrying across the small park on their way home from their jobs.

'Ivan!' A whisper almost at his elbow made Ivan jump.

'Volodia!' Ivan was so surprised, he simply stared.

'Follow me but don't walk together!' Volodia commanded.

'But I'm supposed to meet Mr. Newell...' Ivan protested.

'I know. Come!' Volodia struck off at a brisk pace. His heart beating with excitement, Ivan followed a safe distance behind.

There was a large American car idling at the end of the road along the side of the square. A block ahead, Volodia suddenly dove inside the car.

Ivan sped up his fast walking almost to a run and without even looking inside the car, followed Volodia exactly, opening the back of the car and plunging into the interior.

Instantly the engine accelerated as Mr. Newell tossed greeting to Ivan over his shoulder. 'Good work, Ivan! That was smooth!'

'Keep down, Ivan!' Volodia was hunched in the seat so that his head hardly appeared. Ivan copied his slumped posture.

'Where are we going? Where's Katya? What's happened?' It was dark out now and the graceful street lights threw arches of light onto the road. Ivan peered out of the window of the car.

'Katya's fine and is at my apartment with my wife...' Mr. Newell began.

'And my uncle is there too!' Volodia burst out.

'We're going there, Ivan, but first we have to hide you boys in the trunk of the car. There's been a Russian guard at our gate and you can't be seen.'

'Why are we going there?' Ivan had never been to the apartment of a foreigner. Such an activity would be looked on with great suspicion by the officials.

'Don't be concerned about it, Ivan,' Mr. Newell

said with a grin. 'My wife and I have worked out rather a good system for guests. You won't be seen. It's a good place to talk, and since Katya is there, I thought it would be good if we could all be together to plan. There's certainly no other place in Moscow where a Christian, an escaped poet, a foreign correspondent, and…'

'A circus acrobat!' Volodia added mischievously.

'… can talk together safely.'

The car slowed down by a deserted side of a square. On one side was an unlit stretch of park. Across the road was a government building closed for the night.

'When I stop the car, I will jump out and open the trunk. You boys get out right away and get into the trunk. We are only two or three minutes from where I live. You will be cramped in the trunk, but all right. The guard won't ask me to open it. We'll be home before you know it!' Mr. Newell assured them cheerfully.

Even Volodia looked nervous as he curled up swiftly in his side of the trunk. Ivan pulled his head as far down as possible as the trunk top slammed down. There was more room than he had expected, although it was a very strange feeling to be crouched inside in utter blackness as the car glided around the corner to the foreign apartment complex.

'What if the guard does ask to open the trunk?' Ivan asked urgently.

Volodia's voice was muffled in his clothes. 'Mr. Newell says he won't. And once we are inside in the parking lot, it is safe. The lights there are out. They have not been working for a long time.'

Ivan joined Volodia in a stifled laugh. 'Mr.

Newell said he thinks the foreigners turn them off or break them if the officials ever do get them operating because they don't like being spied on! Mr. Newell's apartment door is right off the parking lot so it's easy to get in.'

'How do you know all this?' Ivan was beginning to feel hot. The car was slowing down.

'I came in and out this way earlier. In with Katya and my uncle. Out to get you.'

'Katya was in the trunk?' Ivan was amazed.

'No. My uncle and I. Katya was under a blanket on the back seat floor. I think Mr. Newell was a little worried about it, but the guard didn't look.'

Suddenly the trunk top flew open so abruptly that both Ivan and Volodia were badly startled.

'Quick!' Mr. Newell pulled Ivan by the arm. Volodia leaped out as if he were on a trapeze and slammed the trunk shut.

The three of them ran to a door. In a flash, Mr. Newell unlocked the door and thrust the boys inside. The room blazed with light.

A Strange Reunion

Before Ivan could get his eyes properly adjusted to the light, Katya hurled herself joyfully into his arms.

'I knew you would get here all right, Ivan!' she exclaimed. She released Ivan and gave Volodia a fierce hug.

Shyly, Ivan took in the scene as Mr. Newell made introductions and got everyone seated in the living room. It was a large room and very comfortably furnished with American furniture and thick carpets on the floor. Ivan liked the pot of spring flowers on the table and glanced at all the English books and magazines that were neatly placed on shelves or tables around the room. On an end table was a Bible. Ivan's first impulse was to warn Mr. Newell that he shouldn't leave his Bible out in plain sight like that, but then he remembered that of course it was all right for foreigners to have Bibles.

Mrs. Newell was younger looking than her husband, Ivan thought. She was dressed in a skirt and sweater, which surprised Ivan. Most American women in tour groups seemed to wear pant suits and Ivan had thought that was how American women dressed. Her blonde hair was short and bouncy and she smiled warmly at Ivan as he sat down.

Ivan was astonished that the man sitting quietly in a chair in the corner was Alexander Ivanovich,

Volodia's uncle! When Mr. Newell introduced him, the poet did not stand up and embrace in the Russian manner. 'I am very happy to meet you, Ivan Sergeivich,' he said softly. 'Please forgive me for not greeting you properly. I am afraid my 'treatments' in the psychiatric hospital have made me a little ill.'

Volodia hovered anxiously around his uncle's chair. 'Mr. Newell thinks it will be only a little while before my uncle is quite recovered from the terrible things they did to him in the hospital.' He looked to Mr. Newell for assurance.

'Oh, yes, Volodia. I am certain!'

Mrs. Newell, her eyes twinkling with pleasure, left the room and returned almost immediately with a tray of Pepsi-Cola bottles balanced carefully beside tall glasses.

'Oh! Pepsi-Cola!' Katya cried rapturously. 'I have had it only once before in my whole life!'

Volodia shrugged. 'It has been sold in Russia for some time now. We have it at the circus sometimes.'

'Well,' Ivan grinned with Katya. 'We don't have it! Thank you, Mrs. Newell.'

Mrs. Newell nodded and passed a plate of cookies.

'These are candy cookies,' Katya exclaimed. 'They have chocolate pieces inside them.'

Ivan took a bite. It tasted as good as anything he had ever eaten. He tried to eat slowly to make it last. Mrs. Newell smiled. 'I hope you like them. They are chocolate chip cookies.'

Mr. Newell was sitting on the edge of his comfortable chair. 'You must have known, Ivan, that something urgent had happened or I would never have contacted you as I did.'

'Yes.' It took only few minutes to catch Ivan up on Katya's adventure up to the time she was walking along the incinerator passageway of the Serbsky.

'I knew I had to unlock the door and hurry away. It wasn't that I got mixed up or anything…'

'It is only that time had run out,' Uncle Sasha said gently. 'I didn't expect Katya's visit with Comrade Orlov to last so long. They lock the ward immediately after visitors' hours and so I had to almost follow Katya down the hall to the outside door that she was to unlock. I slipped out of the ward just in time. The door locked behind me. Then I had to get out of the building. And of course I would be missed right away.'

'So when I unlocked the incinerator door, Volodia's uncle pushed past me so fast to get out, he knocked me over and I hurt my ankle. By this time we were both on the outside of the door…'

'And I had to try to bring her with me.'

'We didn't know what to do, because I could hardly walk. Volodia's uncle had a hiding place on the other side of Moscow, but it was too far away. I thought of coming to Volodia. It was a crazy idea, maybe, but we were closest to the circus.'

'But then, I am supposed to be the madman,' joked Volodia's uncle.

Volodia suddenly burst in. 'When Katya came to the circus, Uncle Sasha was waiting in a small restaurant nearby. I couldn't think of anything to do but call Mr. Newell. I guess we all panicked.'

'It was a good idea,' Volodia's uncle smiled slowly at him.

Ivan glanced at Katya's foot. It was securely wrapped in an elastic bandage.

'I have an American friend who is a doctor,' Mrs. Newell said. 'She looked at it and said it was only a sprain.'

Ivan's head was spinning with a flurry of explanations. 'I think I understand everything that has happened,' he said slowly. 'But now what do we do?'

Mrs. Newell laughed. 'It's a good question. In one small foreign apartment in the heart of Moscow are two Russian Christians who shouldn't be here, one escaped poet, and one charming young acrobat who is usually followed by the KGB.'

'That's right,' Ivan said suddenly. 'Volodia! Weren't you watched? How did you get away from the circus with Katya?'

'Lately I have not been watched much. Just once in a while someone from the police comes along to check on me. It was lucky.'

'I was praying!' Katya grinned.

Instead of the mocking shrug Ivan was expecting from Volodia, he was surprised to see Volodia give Katya a thoughtful nod.

'Now what we do,' said Mr. Newell in answer to Ivan's earlier question, 'is make a new plan that will not fail.'

Volodia suddenly stood up. 'Wherever my uncle goes, I want to go too! I will leave the circus.'

Tears stood in the poet's eyes as he looked at his nephew. 'No, Volodia. You have a rich life ahead...'

Volodia went to his uncle and sat on the arm of his chair looking down at him, also with tears. 'Uncle Sasha, you are the richness of my life. Please let me be with you. You are the only family I have. I will go where you go.' Volodia bent down and embraced his uncle to settle the matter.

The uncle hesitated a moment, then answered softly, 'There is nothing I would love more than for us to be together – if you are sure.'

Volodia laughed. 'I am sure!' But then his face grew grave. 'But a plan…if only I am not so closely watched! Tomorrow night I must perform my trapeze act and also I am helping the clown act. I have to go back to the circus to get my belongings and my money. If only somehow Uncle and I could just leave from this apartment. Now that Uncle Sasha has escaped, I think they will take me in for questioning. But not before the performance. It is the last evening. The officials will wait.'

Katya sighed. 'I have not seen your clown act, Volodia. I wish Ivan and I had seen it.'

'They will let me do my act,' Volodia repeated. 'But afterward it will be difficult to get away.'

'And you will need to do it quickly,' said Mr. Newell. 'Your uncle may stay here and leave directly from my apartment when you are able to get away, Volodia. Another place to stay, even for a night or two, would be too dangerous.'

'Yes,' Ivan agreed thoughtfully. 'Neighbors talk, people see things.'

'But if I go back to the circus, how can I get away from the agents watching me? They are sure to pick me up as soon as the grand finale of the circus is over!'

Ivan caught his breath in excitement and pressed his hands together against his lips. 'I have a plan!' he said.

Volodia's Confession

'But Ivan, it is so dangerous! It is crazy and risky. It would never work!' Volodia exclaimed.

Ivan was sitting back in his chair with a very pleased look on his face. 'It will work, Volodia. It is perfect!'

Mr. Newell glanced at Uncle Sasha. 'I think it will work.'

Katya was frightened. 'Ivan, you are going to dress up in Volodia's clown costume and take his place in the grand finale? You?'

'Of course,' Ivan laughed. 'It is perfect! That will give Volodia time to get away from the circus as soon as he finishes his act and before the circus is over. The agents will be watching me.'

'That's just the point, Ivan,' Volodia protested. 'How will you get away from the agents?'

Ivan shrugged. 'I will have to get to your dressing room, take off the clown costume and pretend I am just a part of the audience. I have come backstage to try to meet one of the performers.'

'It would give Volodia the chance to give the KGB the slip.' Mr. Newell was still looking at Volodia's uncle.

'But it is unsafe for young Ivan.'

'Would Momma and Poppa let you, Ivan?' Katya asked dubiously.

'Momma wouldn't. Poppa might,' Ivan answered.

'I would talk it over with Poppa. I think he will agree. He said Christians are to do good to all men. I know he wants us to help if we can.'

'Why?' the question was distressed. Everyone looked at Volodia. 'Why do you care so much?' Volodia demanded. 'Why should all of you risk so much for my uncle and me?'

There was a stillness in the room. Ivan answered slowly. 'Volodia, all my life I have known that Jesus Christ cares for me. He gave his life so that I could come to God and belong to God. I'm not very good at explaining, but we can't help wanting to help you because if Jesus were here, he would. He loves you.' Ivan finished, feeling a little foolish. He felt he hadn't said it right at all.'

What happened next astonished everyone.

Volodia buried his hands in his face. 'God,' he said. The words were muffled. 'I can't stand any more. I believe in you. You know I believe.'

Mr. Newell pulled his chair closer to Volodia. 'Volodia, I know you believe.'

'I tried to make fun of it all,' Volodia said, his hands still covering his face. 'I tried to pretend. But I knew Ivan and Katya, and even you, Mr. Newell…I knew after a while that when you talked about God and praying and believing, it was real. I felt as if a great space inside myself was wanting to be filled.'

Ivan and Katya sat utterly still, staring at Volodia. Ivan was almost afraid to breathe.

'Volodia!' Mr. Newell spoke softly, but his voice had a hint of a command.

Volodia lowered his hands.

'Volodia, do you want to declare yourself a Christian?'

'Yes.' Volodia looked miserable.

Mr. Newell laughed. 'God will take anybody, Volodia. Even sinners who feel as if coming to him is the end of the world.'

'It's the end of my world!' Volodia declared.

Mrs. Newell gave a smile to Mr. Newell. 'Yes, it is, Volodia. It is the end of many bad things in your world. But it is the beginning of far more than you can know right now. It is the beginning of joy and safety and understanding.'

Volodia smiled sheepishly. 'I'm not sure I know enough to be a Christian.'

'There is a lot to learn,' Mr. Newell agreed. 'But becoming a Christian is not so much to know. You believe in God? That he exists?'

'Of course. I have seen how God answers Katya's prayers.' Volodia's voice became gruff again. 'I have been trying very hard not to believe in God. But I have seen him in Ivan's life, too. And when I learned that you too are a believer, Mr. Newell, an educated man like you, I couldn't say any more that only stupid people could believe in God. I began to feel I was the stupid one.'

'Oh, you're not stupid, Volodia,' Katya protested gently.

'And more than that, one day I realized that if a person believes in God, a lot of things suddenly make sense that didn't make any sense before. It always seemed unbelievable to me that the whole universe 'just happened' – things like that.'

Ivan's eyes were shining. 'Volodia, that's terrific.'

'And all the conversations you had with me, Ivan, about Jesus Christ. Even that first one on the train.

Perhaps you thought I was always making fun, but I was listening!'

Volodia's uncle had turned in his chair and was listening intently to Volodia.

'I used to wonder why people did such terrible things. Why I did things I was ashamed of afterward. Once Ivan talked about everyone being a sinner. That fit too. When I thought about God, I felt like a sinner.'

'I remember the day I talked to you about Jesus dying for our sins.' Ivan smiled at Volodia.

'And I said I didn't want anyone to take any punishment for me. That I was strong enough to take my own!' Volodia shifted restlessly in his chair. 'I only said that because I felt guilty.' Volodia paused a long time. Everyone in the room waited. 'I can't go back to my old way of thinking and living. Everything has changed. I don't really understand it all, but I know I believe.' Volodia looked directly at Ivan. 'Ivan, I've explained all this to God.'

Ivan laughed at the earnest look on Volodia's face. Jumping up from his chair he gave Volodia a hug. 'Oh, Volodia, to think of you praying!'

'Praying?' Volodia looked slightly alarmed.

'Of course!' Ivan's face was still lit by a smile. 'Explaining things to God – that's part of praying, Volodia.'

Volodia looked pleased. 'I was praying and I didn't know it? I must be a Christian!'

'Let's pray now,' Mr. Newell exclaimed. The children and Mrs. Newell agreed with pleasure. For the next few minutes, voices of thanksgiving and praise filled the room.

A Bold Scheme

Mrs. Newell passed mugs of hot soup around the circle. At first Katya had thought it was borscht, but it was not the dark red of the beet soup. It was orange and strange-looking. And there was no sour cream on top. Mrs. Newell also had white bread and butter and jam and hard-boiled eggs. 'It's tomato soup, Katya' Mrs. Newell explained. 'Do you like tomato soup?'

'I don't know,' Katya sniffed the steam delicately. 'It is an unusual color.'

'It's the color of tomatoes,' Ivan declared. 'I am sure it is very good.'

'Well, it's only canned soup. But I hope you'll enjoy it.'

'You have soup in cans?' Katya asked, amazed. 'Is it Canadian soup?'

'Oh, yes, very Western.' Mrs. Newell passed a cup of soup to Volodia's uncle. 'You look very tired,' she said. 'It has been a hard day for you.'

'Yes. It is the treatments they gave me that have left me feeling unwell. But I am sure I will be fine.' He sipped the hot soup with appreciation.

'We have prayed much for the success of Ivan's plan,' Mr. Newell began. 'It depends upon whether his parents agree with Volodia that it is a risk.'

'I know it will work!' Katya declared enthusiastically. 'I am sure Poppa will say yes – Momma, too.'

Ivan looked dubious, but full of resolve.

'First, I will take Ivan and Katya out of the apartment complex in the trunk of the car,' Mr. Newell said. 'Are you sure your ankle is all right, Katya? If I let you off a few blocks from your apartment, can you walk home all right?'

'Certainly!' Katya tossed her braids. 'It is a little sore, but I can easily walk on it now.'

'Then you will talk to your parents and if they agree with the plan, you will be at the circus tomorrow night. It is best not to make any contact before then. If you come to the circus we will know that the plan will be undertaken.'

Ivan nodded.

'Then later tonight, Mrs. Newell and I will go out together for the evening. That time, Volodia will be in the trunk and we will get him back to the circus. We will have to take the chance that KGB agents will not bother him tonight.'

'I am almost sure they will not,' Volodia said thoughtfully. 'Tomorrow my section of the circus goes on tour. If I am prevented from performing, there will be many questions. It is easier just to wait until tomorrow. I think they will.'

'I do too,' said Mr. Newell, putting his cup on the table. 'But now I think it is time for the return of Katya and Ivan. Are you ready?'

The children nodded. After a flurry of goodbye hugs and handshakes, they were huddled in the trunk of the car, hearts pounding from the excitement of rushing to the car and jumping in the trunk as fast as possible. In what seemed like no time, they were standing in their own living room, safe with Momma and Poppa.

It took a long time for Ivan and Katya to explain all that had happened in the past few hours. Poppa listened patiently, his face occasionally breaking into a smile or looking very grave.

Momma was anxious about Katya's ankle and cross that she had gone to the Serbsky Institute. 'It doesn't matter that you didn't want to worry me!' she scolded. 'You must promise me that you will not do such things any more!'

Katya felt sorry that she had upset Momma and was quick to ask her forgiveness. 'I know I don't think sometimes, Momma. I am very sorry. And I will try in future not to behave so thoughtlessly. And perhaps we may go and visit Mr. Orlov again!'

'But Ivan, now what is to be done?' Poppa rubbed his chin reflectively. 'How in the world will Volodia get away from the circus tomorrow night in order to travel with his uncle to some far-away place?'

'And the KGB will find them anyway,' Momma said. 'There's nowhere they will be safe.'

'Mr. Newell said that because his story is now in so many papers in the West, he is sure that even though the KGB may eventually find Volodia and his uncle, they will probably leave him alone. Time will have passed and they won't want to stir up publicity.'

Poppa looked hard at Ivan. 'Well? How is Volodia going to get away from the KGB? I have a feeling, Ivan, that somehow you are going to be involved.'

'Oh, I hope not!' Momma exclaimed.

'I promised I would not do anything without your permission, Momma, Poppa,' Ivan began.

Momma settled back in her chair a little. Poppa looked skeptical. 'But there is a plan?'

Ivan nodded. 'It is quite simple, really. We will all go to the circus tomorrow night…'

'The circus!' Momma was dubious. 'Ivan, I have never in my life been to the circus and neither has your father. For a Christian to attend a circus…' Her voice trailed off for a moment.

'It is to help someone, Momma. It is not for our own pleasure. It is to help a new Christian,' Katya added, suddenly inspired.

Poppa's eyes twinkled playfully. 'And of course Katya will not enjoy one moment of it. She will only endure it to help this 'new Christian.''

Katya grinned. 'I do like the circus, I suppose. But now that I have seen it, I really won't ask to go again.'

'I know you won't, Katushka,' Poppa smiled. 'All right, Ivan, suppose we all go to the circus tomorrow night.'

'Volodia will do his acrobatic act early in the evening and later he has a small part in the clown act. He wears a clown costume and a funny rubbery mask and wig on his head. You would never know it was Volodia!'

Momma nodded, a puzzled frown creasing her forehead.

'The last thing Volodia has to do is to come out for the grand finale march with all the performers, still in his clown costume. That's where the plan comes in.' Ivan paused. Poppa and Momma waited quietly. 'At intermission, I will slip away and go to Volodia's dressing room. I'll wait for him there. When he finishes his clown act, he'll come back to the dressing room, change into street clothes and slip away. I'll put on the clown costume and…uh…' Ivan cleared his throat and finished the end of the sentence in a rush. '…uh…just go out and appear in the grand finale. The KGB will be watching for Volodia and when they see the clown, they won't know he is gone. This will give Volodia a good headstart before the police realize he has run away.'

Momma appealed to Poppa with frightened eyes. Poppa stood up and walked to the window, looking out over the lights of Moscow before he spoke.

'That's fine, Ivan, but I'm sure you've realized that the KGB will be a little surprised when they find you under the clown costume and not Volodia.'

'But they won't find me!' Ivan said. 'As soon as the finale is over, I'll slip into Volodia's dressing room, pull off the clown stuff and come out dressed in street clothes. If there are any agents that see me I can always say I am looking for Volodia.' Ivan glanced at Momma. 'I will be looking for Volodia. I don't want to find him, but I want to see he isn't there.'

'It is very, very dangerous,' Poppa began.

'It is impossible!' Momma declared.

'But it is necessary, Momma. Volodia can't get away otherwise. Since his uncle's escape, the police are sure to bring him in for interrogation and try to use him to get the uncle back.'

'We prayed a lot about it, Momma,' Katya said. 'I am believing God that he will take care of Ivan. After all, God wants Volodia to be able to be free and find other believers and grow in his Christian life. I am sure God will take care of everything and everyone.'

'There is so much confusion backstage,' Ivan said. 'It is not hard to do it.'

'And if someone sees you going into Volodia's dressing room at intermission?' Momma asked.

'That's all right. I am his friend. He has invited me.'

'But the grand finale.' Poppa looked bewildered. 'Ivan, how will you go out in front of all those people? And what will you do? How will you know what to do?'

For the first time, Ivan looked a little nervous. 'Well, that's the part that's a bit tricky. But, I just have to run alongside the other clowns, kicking an imaginary ball in the air and sometimes falling when I catch it. That's all.'

Katya giggled. 'Except you might kick when you're supposed to fall or fall when you're supposed to kick!'

Momma looked so flabbergasted, Ivan laughed. 'Momma, I'll be all right. Momma, Poppa, may I do it? I really think it will work.'

Poppa looked at Momma. Momma shook her head helplessly. 'It's up to you, Sergei. Things seem to have gone so far…'

'We are all praying, Poppa,' Katya volunteered. 'I know God will keep Ivan safe.'

Poppa was quiet a long time. Ivan knew he was trying to sense what the Lord wanted him to say. Finally he rumpled Ivan's hair playfully.

'Well, Ivan,' he said, 'you've always been a bit of a clown, anyway. Let's see how you do!

Volodia's Triumph

Even Poppa was smiling at Momma's nervousness as they entered the circus building. 'Natasha,' he grinned. 'You are not worried so much about the KGB as about being at the circus!'

'Shhh!' Momma looked at him with a glint of humour. 'This is worldly, Sergei. I know we are doing it to help Volodia, but it is not where I would choose to go.'

'We know, Momma.' Ivan was the first to give his ticket to the old woman who stood at the entrance to the auditorium, Katya eagerly at his heels. 'Come on, Momma! Poppa!'

They sat down in four seats near an aisle exit. Ivan looked around casually. Dotted among the earlycomers were bored-looking men he knew were KGB agents.

Ivan was looking at the exit and measuring how much time at intermission it would take him to get backstage to Volodia's dressing room. His heart pounding as he thought of all that would have to be accomplished before they were all safe again at home that evening.

Finally the lights of the auditorium dimmed to black and the giant screen was lowered from the ceiling just as before. Momma gasped in wonder and Ivan and Katya smiled at each other in pleasure. Patriotic pictures flashed again on the screen as the circus troupe began marching into the ring, accompanied by the heroic music of the orchestra. Flags flew, horses cantered, clowns somersaulted, bears lumbered along linked to their costumed trainers by silver chains. In the ring immediately in front of the Nazaroffs, an elephant, resplendent in an immense sparkling saddle, trumpeted a loud elephant shriek. Katya laughed out loud in delight.

To Ivan, it was like a wonderful dream that one knows is about to turn into a nightmare. In the dream, everything is beautiful and enjoyable, but the dreamer is gripped, all the same, with a feeling of terror. The sleeper's sense of some dreadful event just about to occur was upon him.

Poppa glanced at Ivan and gave him a reassuring squeeze on the arm, but his gesture was interrupted by Katya's gasp, 'Oh, it's Volodia! He is the first act tonight!'

On a platform high above the circus floor, in what appeared to be a tangle of ropes and bars, stood the figure of Volodia, dressed in an electric-blue costume. The master of ceremonies was announcing his act. In a second, Volodia made a leap and was flying in great swoops back and forth from one side of the circus roof clear across to the other. Spotlights caught perfectly the lightning-like twists of his body as he leaped from one swinging bar to another. The audience was breathless.

Both of Momma's hands were on her heart. She watched Volodia in speechless horror.

Even some of the other acrobats appeared, clustering around the entrances to the rings to watch Volodia's spectacular performance. It was as if every restraint on his spirit was gone and he was free, as few mortals ever are, to defy space and fear. The audience began applauding in the thundering, rhythmic Soviet way long before Volodia's act was finished. When he took his bows on the circus floor, the applause was deafening. Gracefully, Volodia turned and ran from the ring. The rest of the performances were a blur to Ivan. Suddenly, the ringmaster announced the intermission.

Katya swallowed hard as Ivan pulled on his jacket to go. Poppa always calm under pressure, stretched a little. 'How about some ice cream?' he asked loudly, his eyes resting for a brief and reassuring moment on Ivan.

Momma nodded. Ivan knew she was being very brave. He knew she was fighting down the impulse to hang onto his arm, to ask him not to go.

'Yes, I'd like some.' The blood was pounding in Ivan's ears. Katya's voice sounded strange.

'I'm going backstage to say hello to Volodia, if I can,' Ivan said.

The rest of the family nodded and filed out with the crowds to the refreshment booths.

Backstage, all was activity. A team of workers had just expertly rolled up the huge mat in one of the rings and were heaving it onto their shoulders to exchange it for another mat for the acts to follow the intermission. Musicians were milling about, some smoking, some forming lines for cold drinks backstage.

Ivan glided through the performers rapidly. No one seemed to bother about him. He knew exactly where he was going. One knock on Volodia's door and the door swung open. Volodia yanked Ivan into the room and shut and locked the door.

'Oh, Volodia, you were wonderful!' Ivan stared at his friend in admiration.

Volodia was pulling off the blue costume with absolute concentrated speed, pushing his feet into the pants of a garishly colored clown outfit. 'You stay here,' he was saying to Ivan. 'As soon as the clown act is over, I'll come back and you can have the costume.' Volodia stopped dead in his rapid action. 'Ivan, are you all right?'

'I think so,' Ivan said. 'It's just that I'm not sure I can pull it off. What if someone finds out it's not you?'

Volodia continued to wriggle into his costume. 'No time to think about that now, Ivan!' he exclaimed cheerfully. 'Besides, I know God will take care of us.'

Ivan took a deep breath. Just having Volodia, of all people reassuring him about God's care quieted him. 'I know it too, Volodia.'

'You just have to move very fast, Ivan, and keep moving. As soon as you see Rotman and Makovsky, join them. Move fast!'

'But they are so famous…'

'Right! They are the most famous clowns in the Soviet Union. Everyone will be watching them – not you!'

'And as soon as the last bow is taken, I will come back here, change, get out of your dressing room, get back to my parents, and leave.'

'Simple!' Volodia thumped Ivan on the back. 'Ivan, I will never forget what you are doing. I am sorry there is no time to say it properly.'

'God go with you,' Ivan said, his voice husky.

And with you!' Volodia embraced Ivan. 'Uncle is

already waiting for me in the car of a friend. We will be away from the circus as soon as my act is over and long enough before the finale.'

'Katya will watch at the front of the circus. Will you try and wave to her? So we will know?'

'I will try.' Volodia pulled a grinning clown's mask over his head. It was a mask topped with curly black hair. He jumped playfully and tripped in front of Ivan. Ivan laughed. 'Get going, Volodia. I will wait here until your act is over.'

Volodia paused at the door. 'Lock it. Don't answer it. When I come, I will give two raps and then two more raps. Open it then.' In a flash he was gone and Ivan was left alone with his pounding heart and the faint starting up of the vigorous circus music in the far distance of the centre ring.

A New Beginning

When Ivan, in days to come, was to look back on those minutes in Volodia's dressing room, they would become, each time he remembered them, more and more like a dream. It seemed to him no time at all until Volodia's knocks were sounding at the door and Volodia plunged into the room, ripping off the mask and the clown outfit. Ivan could see then that Volodia was fearful. His face was strained and white and he took much longer than Ivan thought he ought to have taken in gathering his few belongings, checking his papers and money, and disappearing out of the room. His goodbye hug to Ivan had been tense.

But as Ivan waited nervously in the ludicrous clown costume, sweating under the unaccustomed confinement of the mask, time seemed to stand still. Over and over Ivan was seized with panic that he had somehow missed the grand finale. It became harder and harder to tell, after fanfares, if it were the end of the circus or only the end of an act. Once, unable to restrain his tension, he opened Volodia's door a crack, sure the troupe was assembling backstage for the finale, only to see a few trainers and animals waiting for their act to begin.

Finally, there was a great commotion in the backstage area. The orchestra struck up a very loud and slow fanfare. It was the finale! Ivan heaved open the door and ran out of the dressing room with such speed he fell into a small family group of acrobats arranging themselves in order for the curtain call.

'Volodia! What's the matter with you?' the woman exclaimed irritably. 'You almost knocked me over. Get out there. Makovsky's about to go on!'

Ivan twisted through the performers, looking ahead to the famous pair of clowns about to run into the ring. A blast of trumpets and the two clowns, not even looking back for him, tumbled into the ring. Ivan fell after them, slipping in the huge shoes that were part of Volodia's costume. The crowd roared in appreciation.

Makovsky glanced over his shoulder in mild interest and continued his pace around the huge ring, bowing and producing his final antics to delight the crowd. Ivan kept a little distance behind the two master clowns, as Volodia had advised, bowing and occasionally somersaulting, kicking an imaginary ball, and jumping in imitation of the professional clowns. Ivan was thankful for the exercises he had to do as a soccer player. It was easy for him to clown.

Anxiously, Ivan tried to see into the crowds. All was a blur. Passing an exit, he did notice one of the men he had thought to be a KGB agent observe him carefully as he danced past.

They are going to come after me as soon as the finale is over! Oh, God, give me enough time…Ivan's eyes were on the exit. The crowd was applauding, stamping their feet in pleasure at the last moments of the spectacle before them.

Suddenly Ivan felt perfectly calm and alert. Even as he leaped and bowed and danced he could see he would gain precious seconds by being close to the edge of the ring rather than in the centre of the performers who were exiting as they came to the end of their finale. Edging over to the side, Ivan made a great bow and, looking up, caught a flash of Katya's face. Her expression seemed to be either complete rapture or complete terror. Ivan couldn't tell which and there wasn't time to think about it.

The exit loomed in front of him. It would be a few more moments before he would be out of the sight of the audience. As soon as he had passed into the hall, Ivan moved like lightning toward Volodia's room.

Before he had the door opened, he had unhooked his huge costume belt. Entering the room, and slamming the door shut, he kicked off the floppy shoes and pulled off the mask and wig in the same movement. It seemed to him only an instant before he was again in the hall, in his own clothes, and in the middle of the troupe making their way to dressing rooms.

Ivan made for the exit to the auditorium again as if for his life. A huge hand grabbed him by the shoulder and held him.

'What do you think you're doing?'

Ivan expected to see the sallow face of a KGB agent. Instead, the huge red face of the circus master loomed above him.

'I'm sorry!' Ivan was so genuinely afraid his voice shook. He tried to steady it. 'I…I wanted to, uh…I know someone who works in the circus…I wanted to, uh…see if he was in his dressing room.'

'Who?' the circus master demanded.

Ivan was speechless. The man shoved him toward the exit. 'A likely story! You've got no business here, boy! Out you go!' He shoved Ivan through the exit into the auditorium.

Only a few people were still leaving their seats. Ivan could not see Momma or Poppa or Katya anywhere. Hurrying toward the public exit, he got out into the large entrance hall, past the ice cream booth that was doing a brisk business, and to the main doors of the circus.

His eye caught Katya's wave. As he approached her, her arm shot out and without a word she yanked Ivan through the doors into the street.

The spring evening was warm and wet. Momma and Poppa were waiting for Ivan. Momma's face was shining with joy. Poppa was beaming.

Katya hugged Ivan. 'He's safe, Ivan! I saw the car and Volodia and his uncle drive by. He waved to me.'

Momma was hurrying the family group away from the circus doors and toward the bus stop. Crocuses, like the ones Katya had taken to Mr. Orlov, were pushing up through the damp earth of the walkway along the sidewalk. Katya shuddered for an instant, remembering the hospital and the dreadful sufferings of Volodia's uncle and Christian believers too.

'Ivan! Ivan!' There were running footsteps. Ivan turned to see Mr. Newell pushing his way through the crowds on the street. 'Thanks to God! he said in his awkward Russian, his excitement blurring the usually good pronunciation.

Momma and Poppa were laughing. 'Yes, thanks be to God.'

'I saw them in the car!' Katya declared excitedly. 'I saw them drive by!'

'So did I,' Mr. Newell. 'I was watching from the other side of the building. No one will bother them now.'

'Are you sure?' Poppa had resumed walking and the happy group fell in with him.

'I am sure,' Mr. Newell said, still talking excitedly and making them all smile at his Russian. 'There has been so much publicity in the West about the case, the Russian authorities will be glad to leave them well enough alone.'

At the bus stop, there was another small planting of crocuses, making a yellow patch under the street light. Everyone was quiet for a moment, conscious of people around them also waiting for the bus.

'It's a sign of new life,' Katya said, looking at the flowers.

'Yes.' Momma and Poppa smiled warm, deep smiles. 'A whole new life.'

Mr. Newell put an arm around Ivan. His eyes twinkled. 'Well, Ivan, it's not every boy who gets to do what you did tonight!'

Ivan grinned. 'That's right. I don't suppose I'll forget this night at the Moscow Circus.'

'Especially the clown act,' Katya grinned, as the bus slowly came to a stop.

'Most especially the clown act,' Ivan agreed. As they climbed onto the bus, they were all smiling.

IVAN SERIES

Before these books were written Russia was a communist country, which meant that belief in God and meeting together to worship him were strictly forbidden. Because of this, Russian Christians had to meet in secret. They had to be very careful of what they said and whom they trusted. Otherwise they could face arrest, interrogation, imprisonment, torture and sometimes even death.

As you read these books you will learn the meaning of some Russian words such as:

Babushka	Grandmother
Tovarisch	Comrade or friend
Kopeks/rubles	Russian money
Pravda	Russian Newspaper
Piroshki	Small, meat-filled rolls
Lobio	Spicy red beans
Borscht	Soup

The Young Pioneers were the Communist Party organization which provided all camping, athletic, musical and cultural activities for Soviet children aged 9-14.

The initials KGB were the initials of Russian Secret Police.

THE IVAN SERIES

These books will have you on the edge of your seat as you enter a different culture, a historical period, and world of just 30 years ago… but Christian children in any era or country will identify with Ivan and Katya's struggles to stay faithful. But they also have to tackle persecution… the separation from families, the interrogations and injustice of a communist society.

Ivan and the Moscow Circus
Read how a key, a car, a foreign journalist and a clown suit help Ivan in one of his greatest adventures

Ivan and the Daring Escape
Ivan is trying to outwit the Secret Police, his skill at football helps him and his friends to get the better of them

Ivan and the Informer
Ivan is taken for questioning and knows there is an informer somewhere – how can he clear his name?

Ivan and the Hidden Bible
Ivan's not the most popular boy in school but he's the best footballer! He and Katya have a holiday on the family farm - will they find their Grandfather's hidden Bible?

Ivan and the Secret in the Suitcase
Here are Ivan and Katya in another adventure – Smuggling! Can they outwit the secret police?

Ivan and the American Journey
Ivan has won a prize in history and travels to the USA it is a journey full of adventure and intrigue.

CHRISTIAN FOCUS PUBLICATIONS

Christian Focus   **Christian Heritage**   **CF4K**   **Mentor**

Christian Focus Publications publishes books for adults and children under its three main imprints: Christian Focus, Mentor and Christian Heritage.

Our books reflect that God's word is reliable and Jesus is the way to know him, and live for ever with him. Our children's publication list includes a Sunday school curriculum that covers pre-school to early teens; puzzle and activity books.

We also publish personal and family devotional titles, biographies and inspirational stories that children will love. If you are looking for quality Bible teaching for children then we have an excellent range of Bible story and age specific theological books.

From preschool to teenage fiction, we have it covered!

Find us at our webpage:
www.christianfocus.com

CF4·K
Because you're never
to young to know Jesus